Dedication

George Burras Jr. & Mary Ann Burras
Who raised me to be extraordinary

Jason, Jayla & Jaiden Holmes
Who needs to see their mom being extraordinary so they
not only know what extraordinary looks like, but also
that it's possible.

Preface

Before I knew what I was doing I was barging into the room yelling for this mother fucker to get his mother fucking hands off my mother fucking wife. Startled! He jumped! Without allowing him to process a second thought, I was already in his vicinity with my right hand balled into the tightest fist I could muster flying directly towards his face. The next three punches landed in his face before he began to defend himself. I don't know if he was severely caught off guard and wasn't able to process what was happening to him or what, but in this moment of clarity I was 100 percent clear on what's been going on. This mother fucker has been smiling in my face all the while sleeping with my wife and I'm about two seconds from killing his bitch ass.

He got in a hard lick to the right side of my jaws. This just pisses me off more. Filled with rage, the room faded into this dark grey hole with black shadows. All I could see is betrayal and anger wearing the face of my wife and this mother fucker. All I feel is the need to cause them the kind of pain they've caused me. I swung every punch with the a force I wasn't even aware I possessed until this very moment. I needed him to feel

the kind of pain that makes you wish you were dead.
The kind of pain so severe, your mind is unable to
process what to do with it. Where to place it. How to
stop it. Every punch I threw towards his body was
accompanied with the vision of this son of a bitch crying
over my wife's bed. He shed tears as if he were afraid of
losing her. Like his heart were shattered. The kind of
tears a man cries when he is looking the loss of his soul
right in the eye and he has no idea how he's going to
cope with that loss. He cried for her as if he were me. As
if he were her husband. He cried the tears that only I
should be crying. Tears that told me everything I needed
to know the moment I saw them.

My wife. My soul. My haven. My peace. My friend.
The woman I would lay down my life for. The only woman
I would lay my life down for. I just cannot imagine a
moment where the woman I love was able rationalize this
level of deceit and engaged in an act she knew would
crush my core. On what planet? At what time? Under
what circumstances did this feel right to her? My pain is
very real and very evident right now, but it is being
overridden by my anger. Anger consumed me at the
thought of the lying, the disrespect, the callousness.
Anger swallowed me at the thought of the most
important person in my life having zero regard for me,

while I have had nothing but the utmost love, respect and consideration for her. This hurt almost cripples me. This mother fucker is about learn what it feels like to feel this kind of pain. So is my wife.

Alicia

I couldn't have asked for a better day. Work is…
Well, work. But productive. I love my students.
I'm always in awe of how intrigued they are with
the material. All of their questions and comments always
spark an interesting class discussion, which is my
motivation to keep the class interesting. Thank God I
don't have to sit through class after class of half asleep,
uninterested, rather-be-anywhere-but-here students
like some of the other professors.

I have a meeting with Dean Kline this afternoon. I
pray she's in a good mood today and open to my
proposal of adding a Black History Enrichment study to
the curriculum. Although Hillcroft's student body is
made up of majority White students, I still feel as though
learning the history of civilization is imperative to all
people, of all races, and not just the responsibility of
Black kids. It's a bold move, but I like to think of myself
as a bold professor. I wouldn't be doing myself or these
kids any favors by not pushing the envelop when the
need arises. I didn't get to where I am by sitting around
taking orders from other people and not being able to
think for myself. Any shot I get to ameliorate the quality

of my students' lives, or at the very least their education, I'm going to take it. I can remember a time back in college when this group of students were rallying in front of the dean's office for the cafeteria to serve more of what's referred to as soul food and foods of that sort. They felt as though the university was not being fair by not considering their needs. Somehow, my roommate and a couple of my other friends had joined in with this group of protestors. They would try their best to persuade me into joining them. Now don't get me wrong, I love mac & cheese, collard greens and cornbread just as much as the next person. I just didn't need it in my life every day, so I didn't feel the need for an all out protest. Therefore, I didn't participate. They attacked me with the assumption that just because I'm African American that it should have been a no brainer and I should have been eager to join them. Most people would have folded under the stares, name-calling and other rude comments that I received when the protestors saw me and a few other nonparticipating Black students ignoring their protests for the cafeteria They were a rather militant group. After several days of the protestors' disrespect, I walked right up to the group with my own bullhorn and informed them that being impertinent was no way to encourage anyone to join their cause. In addition to the fact that they would make the conjecture that simply because we all shared the privilege of having melanin in common that that would somehow make me an automatic candidate for their cause was a form of stereotypical racism in its own right. I reminded them that their actions were the equivalent to someone presumptuously thinking all Black people eat chicken and watermelon. I asked the question how would they feel if someone assumed that just because their skin was darker that they were always up to no good, or that they were feebleminded and lacked common sense. I could see that my comments had gotten their attention. I then suggested that if they wanted the dean to take them seriously, instead of simply protesting loudly and antagonizing students unwilling to jump on their bandwagon, maybe they should put together a formal letter stating their desires, select a leader, and have them set up a meeting with the dean to have open and clear discourse about it. They took my advice. The dean and the students agreed on one day a week. Every Wednesday there would be something soulful on the cafeteria's menu. I like to think I taught them something that day.

****

I sent my husband, Derek, a quick text letting him know I would be a little late getting home. I told him I was staying late to grade papers and afterwards I would be going for a run. Because I didn't get my morning run in, I decided to enjoy the last of this beautiful day by going for a run through the park. Where most people despised the thought of running, I needed to run. When I'm running, that's my time to clear my head, quiet distracting thoughts and gain perspective on situations that may be troubling me. Running is my own form of meditation. I sleep better at night and I'm a happier person during the day when I run. After grading the last of my papers, I got changed into my black running pants, pink tank top and rainbow colored Adidas. I tossed my bag with the clothes I wore to work, along with my heels, into the trunk of my car. I started to stretch in the parking lot next to my car. Because the university is located right next to the park, I decided to leave my car parked in the lot and sprint from there. Armed with my iPod in my armband, my wireless earbuds and my running music geared up, I was ready to go. I locked my phone in the glove compartment of my car, pulled my locks back into a ponytail, and took off. I often took the same route through the park because I enjoyed the scenery. On an afternoon like today, you could easily spot families picnicking, folks walking or playing fetch with their dogs, children laughing and running, college students studying under the trees and kites in the sky. I loved the atmosphere of the park. I often think it lends the perfect background to a photo shoot. Especially when the sky is clear and blue, the sun is bright and the clouds are white as snow. The clean crisp air began to fill my lungs as I began to pick up speed. By the time my arms had begun to sweat, I was in a good place and feeling good. I ran past an old couple holding hands on a bench and thought about my husband. Lord knows I love that man. Although he's the sexiest man alive to me, it's his brilliance and compassion that turns me on most of all. We normally run together on Saturday mornings. Even though running is my time away to escape for a little while, I absolutely love sharing that part of me with him. The times we run together seem to grow our connection somehow. We don't typically do a lot of talking on these runs, which is what I believe makes the runs that much more special; the idea that we can communicate and connect without saying a word. Every now and then, I would miss him when I am running by myself, but today I'm content in my solitude.

****

Now back at my car, I grabbed my phone from the glove compartment and called my honey. The sound of his sexy voice awakens certain parts of me every time I hear it. He has the most seductive baritone I've ever heard in my life. It reminds me of Michael McCary of Boyz II Men.

"Hey, what are you up to?"

"Nothing much, just about to hop in the shower. What are you up to?"

"Just finishing my run. Five miles. I could really use a shower, myself, right about now."

"Luckily for you, there's room for two. With a little persuasion, I may be willing to share it with you."

"Well, you know I do my best persuading in person."

"I'm all too familiar with your ability to influence."

I laughed

"I'll see you shortly."

****

Hours later and I can still taste him. I can still feel his gentle suction on my lips. I keep telling myself that I'm going to leave him alone one day, but that day never comes. Every time I think of his caramel skin touching mine, his beautiful smile and look into those captivating eyes of his it gets harder and harder to do. He's the only man that can send an electric tingle through my entire body with the slightest touch; the most subtle brush of his skin on my skin. I'll never admit it out loud, but I think I love him. Or maybe I just love what he does to me and how he makes me feel. The only thing I am completely sure of is we have the most incredible chemistry. He knows what I'm thinking before I can say it. He's the most understanding, considerate, and comical man I know. I can talk to him about just about anything. One of my favorite things to do is to lie next to him in bed and share our thoughts and feelings. Sometimes, on a night like tonight, I'll lay next to him and just watch him sleep wondering what would it feel like to wake up to his perfect face in the morning; what he would look like with new sun rays gently covering his handsome face just before his eyes flutter and he wakes up to a new day. Knowing that I may never get the chance to find out, I slip out of his bed, get dressed and head home.

Derek

I heard the alarm beep. I called downstairs, "Babe, is that you?"

"Yeah."

"How was your run?"

"It was freeing. Nothing like an afternoon run to release the stress the day brings."

A moment later I'm greeted by my wife with an endless flood of kisses.

"If I didn't know any better I'd say someone missed me."

"I did! How was your day?"

"Great! I finally caught a break today. After weeks of dispositions, finally the firm's investigator obtained the one piece of exculpatory evidence that will prove my client's innocence. The D.A. filed a motion to suppress it, but the judge rejected her request. Looks like Mr. Banks will be a free man."

"That's awesome, babe! I know how taxing this case has been on you. You've been tossing in your sleep all week. Maybe you should make time for a run before Saturday."

"Sorry if I've been keeping you awake, I just couldn't shake the fact that if we could not find what we needed, an innocent man would spend most of his adult life behind bars. I have some time tomorrow morning before work, I think I'll squeeze a few miles in before I head to the office."

"Good! I've been resting just fine, but maybe we both can get some sleep now."

I kissed my wife's forehead before walking over to my dresser to remove my watch and empty my pockets of my wallet, cell phone and a Post-It reminding me to stop at the store on my way home from work to pick up more almond mild and eggs. I don't know why I even bother leaving myself notes because nine times out of 10 I'm going to forget once the note is out of sight.

"How was your day?"

"Constructive. I met with Dean Kline to discuss the addition of my new Black History study. I want to take a much-needed step outside of the normal curriculum and give the privileged students of Hillcroft University a different perspective on history, than what they typically grow up learning in school."

"How did that go?"

"It went rather well. Angela loved my proposal. She thought the idea was refreshing, and welcomed the diversity it would give the students. Now all she has to do is get the board's approval. Let's hope they find it as purposive as she does."

"Well, I'm happy for you, babe. I know that once you set your sights on something you feel passionately about, you won't allow anything or anyone to stand in your way."

I love how ardent my wife is about her work. I think she gets a certain fulfillment out of leaving an impression on those kids. A plethora of people never get to do what they love. Which is highly unfortunate, because it certainly is a liberating feeling knowing you're not just here imitating a Stepford Wife going through your days with no real meaning or purpose.

Glancing over my shoulder I asked, "What do you feel like eating?"

Scrunching her face up as if she were eliminating options in her head Alicia replied, "I think I'm in the mood for Chinese."

"Chinese it is."

I picked up my iPhone and ordered our favorite Chinese food. Although, the both of us are excellent cooks and often love cooking together. Today, has been one of those days I don't want to have to pick up the task of cooking, nor do I want to burden my wife with it. I just want the easy pleasure of her company.

Alicia and I met in college. I guess you could say we're college sweethearts, although we did spend some time apart after college. After about five years of living separate lives, we found our way back to each other. I was pleasantly surprised to find that she was still just as fine as I remembered. She was always the most beautiful woman in a room. The moment I first laid eyes on her, I thought she reminded me of a young Aunt Viv. Her dark skin was flawless. She was so intelligent, sophisticated and inspiring, not to mention she possessed the baddest curves on the planet with just the faintest sliver of hood. I loved that shit. I used to not be able to keep my hands off of her. Hell, what am I talking about? I still can't keep my hands off of her. Alicia hasn't aged a bit. Still the most beautiful woman in any room and the sexiest. I often joke with her that she drinks Benjamin Button water. The only thing that had changed on her was her hair. When we were in school she wore her hair relaxed and tracked just like most of the other sisters on campus. Now she rocks these beautiful long locks, which I prefer. Don't get it twisted, she was just as stunning with the relaxed hair, but it's something bold, remarkable and dignifying about seeing a sister proudly wearing her hair in its natural state.

Once our dinner arrived, I opened a bottle of wine and we sat on the living room floor in front of the coffee table, like kids, watching our recordings of Shonda Rhimes's Thursday night line-up. We don't always have a lot of time for frivolous things, with our demanding careers and maintaining what some would consider healthy social lives. Still, we strive to get in a day a week where we can just turn work off, unplug from family and friends, and all the other crap life throws our way, and just focus on the little things. Tonight that includes takeout, wine, Grey's Anatomy, Scandal and How To Get Away With Murder.

Derek

"They ain't ready! They ain't ready!" Amir yelled after stealing the ball from Rob and tossing me up an alley-oop. We try to meet up at the basketball court whenever we can. Amir has been like my brother for years. I've known him about as long as I've known my wife. We all went to college together. Amir has always had a thing for my sister-in-law, Melissa, but these days Melissa is a happily married woman with two beautiful children. Not that that stops him from trying.

Most of the guys that hang out at the court are younger than us, but that doesn't stop us from getting out there and showing those young boys how a couple of 35 year olds can cut up. As I get older, looking old and out of shape has never been anything that interested me. I enjoy working out and staying fit, and I love that my wife loves the results. She's always so beautiful and walking around sexy as hell, I have to match her sexy. I can't be that guy you see on the street with the beautiful wife and you wonder How in the world did he get her? So I've got to stay on top of my game. At the park, on the court, is my time away from the stress work brings. Amir and I get out here and act out like Wesley Snipes and Woody Harrison in White Men Can't Jump. The new guys always underestimate us until one of us sinks the first three-pointer or the first slam-dunk goes up in one of their faces; which is what's taking place right now. We usually play game after game of two on two or three on three, depending how many guys are at the park ready to play. Today is a light day, so Amir and I are teamed up against two young guys neither of us have seen play here before. One of the guys reminds me of John Sally. He looks like he can play, but I never make assumptions out here, because I know all too well how quick you can make an ass of yourself by assuming the wrong thing. Many guys have made the assumption that we're too old to still be any good on the court, and we have sent many asses walking back to the sidelines scratching their heads with that I can't believe this shit expression on their faces.

There's plenty of girls here today, as well. It's always a few chicks hanging around either watching their man play or here with their friend watching her man play. Although I love my wife and am not looking to go home with any of these women, I must admit, the attention is flattering. It feels good knowing I still got it. Even if it is all for my wife.

I'm having a good time today with my brother. Life couldn't be better than this. Hanging out with my best friend, doing what we love. Then I get to go home to a gorgeous woman who I know loves me unconditionally. But before I do, Amir and I have some unfinished business, "21-14 game point! Who got next?"

After three straight games, Amir and I take a break to give some of the other guys a chance to play. Sitting on the side, I take a few swallows of my Gatorade and check my phone. There's a missed call from the office and a text message from Alicia. I read the message before returning the missed call.

Wifey: Just thinking of you 🥰

Me: I love you. You know that right?

Wifey: You better 😊

Me: What are you up to?

Wifey: Still walking the mall with Mel

Me: How many?

Wifey: How many what?

Me: How many pairs of shoes?

Wifey: Two

Me: Only two?

Wifey: Well don't sound so surprised

Me: 😁 I'm sorry baby. I can't wait to see them.

Wifey: And I can't wait to show them to you. Bossy Mel is insisting I put my phone away. I'll see you later husband

Me: 😘 See you later beautiful

I looked up to see Amir looking at me with his lips twisted up on one side, What's wrong with you?

How many years has it been? And you two still text each other and talk on the phone like you're in high school.

Don't hate on my relationship brother. You could have one too, but you're too busy chasing after a woman you know is unattainable.

Melissa is attainable. Or at least she would be once she loses that guy that's always hanging around her.

You mean her husband? The father of her children? That guy?

Potayto potahto.

We both laugh and drink more Gatorade.

Alicia

F lying across the bridge, music blasting, I'm lost in the excitement of the music and seeing my honey.

We're made of the same stuff as the moon and the
stars
The ocean's salt water just like my tears are
You feel me, the sun rises and sets every day
without fail
That's how I know that God is real
All of this is not by chance

"COME ON INDIA!", I yell out as if she could somehow hear me. I can't help myself though, she speaks to my soul every time she opens her mouth. I can't help but to get caught up in what she's saying and how her music makes me feel. That's exactly what must have happened. I got caught up. Because until this moment I did not notice the police in the SUV parked in one of the forks of the bridge. I tried to press on my brakes and quickly slow down, but I was too late and we both knew it. I knew my Audi had already sent his radar gun into a frenzy. There were no other cars around me. They were all in my rearview. He had no choice but to pull me over and give me a ticket.

"Shit! Shit! Shit!", I promised my husband I wouldn't get anymore tickets. "Shit!" After I drove past him, for some reason, he did not come after me right away. He did that pregnant pause the police do before they hit their lights and speed up to get behind you, where they sit just long enough for you to think maybe he won't pull me over and give me a ticket. Maybe he wasn't sitting out here pointing his speed gun at unsuspecting drivers as they came around the curve of the bridge. Only his pause was just long enough for me to not only think that, but believe it. Was he giving me a pass because I slowed down? Did his radar detect some other speed demon I wasn't aware of? Had he run out of gas sitting in that fork for who knows how long? Whatever the cause for his pause, I thank God for it. By the time I made it to the bottom of the bridge I caught a glimpse of him in my review mirror pulling into the right lane. Immediately after, I saw his lights flashing from the roof of his SUV. Concealed by the exit ramp, after exiting the bridge I quickly made a sharp turn into a busy parking lot next to a large van which concealed my car. I watched as the cop sped down the street with his lights matching his speed. My heart pounded out of my chest. I was so scared. I had no idea I was going to do that until I had already done it. What do I do now? Do I sit here a little longer? Do I pull out into traffic and be on my way? Where is he? Was he chasing after another speeding car and I was just being paranoid?

"OK, Alicia, breathe. Just calm down and think", I said to myself out loud.

I decided to go ahead and take my chances blending in with traffic. A truck paused to let me in and I pulled out onto the busy boulevard. On a busy street lined with business after business, establishment after establishment, my worst fear came true. The police officer was parked two businesses down facing on coming traffic. Lights still flashing. I'm panicked. Hoping he doesn't see me, I gradually float over the middle lane into the far left lane. Red light. Now I'm even more panicked. Did he see me? Is he turning his SUV around to give chase? I just wanted to see my honey. That's all I wanted to do. I have a couple hours before my husband gets home from work, and I just wanted to spend them with my honey. Is this a sign that I need to turn around and go my behind back home? The light's green now. The busyness of this street is shredding my nerves right now, but I guess I ought to be thankful at the same time because I believe it's that same busyness that's saving my butt right now. I catch a few more red lights, but am finally able to turn off of the busy boulevard and into my honey's neighborhood.

Although I was relatively certain I was in the clear, I couldn't help but to continue to check my rearview mirrors for those flashing lights. A few turns later I pulled into my honey's driveway. I was home, safe and ticketless. Thank God. I gathered my purse and keys and swiftly walked up the pathway that led to my honey's front door. As soon as he opened the door, I jumped into in his arms and wrapped my legs around his waist. I haven't seen this man in what feels like forever and I've missed him something serious. I kissed him like I meant it. Like it would be my last time. He held on to me tightly as he kicked the front door closed with his foot and carried me through his living room and down the hall to his bedroom. He laid me on his bed gently. I was excited because I knew what came next. During my moments of clarity, I sometimes feel guilty for indulging in what I know deep down to be wrong. I feel angst in my belly for the outright betrayal of it all. Then I'm pulled back into the allure of it all. I'm addicted to the passion I share with this man. I love my husband, and we share a certain passion between us, but what I have with this man is more of an obsession. I'm drawn to him, and he to me. The way that he wants me makes me want him more. If I could walk away, I would. But every time I try, I'm pulled back into an exhilarating whirlwind of crazed excitement with him. I see fireworks when I'm with him.

I stared back into his eyes as he unzipped my boots and slid them from my feet. I'm not even thinking about the intense journey over here. My body tensed up once he began to slide my jeans off from the anticipation of what was coming. Aroused, I pulled his shirt over his head and kissed his chest. I could never get enough of him. How could it be that I'm so intensely and unmistakably in love with my husband, yet this man awakens parts of me I had no idea existed? His ability to reach areas of my body and mind that Derek has never been able to and cause mini explosions in his wake is astonishing, and somewhat addictive. Until the day I'm able to free myself of his grasp, I'm going to revel in the intense sensations he sends through my body.

Alicia

I absolutely love spending time with my sister. It seems like the older we get the busier we get. And the less we get to see each other. But when your sister is your best friend, you find the time. You make time. I can remember us fighting like cats and dogs growing up. I use to wish that she belonged to another family that lived some place else. Anywhere else. So long as she wasn't around to annoy me. But these days I can't imagine my life without her. I don't know what that would even look like. Who would I call in the middle of the night to talk when I can't sleep? Who would I go shopping with? Who would play hooky with me and sneak off to the movie theater in the middle of the day? Who would have me laughing so hard my spleen hurts? Who would I talk to about the complications of my life while I'm getting my pedicure? I can't think of a soul. She's irreplaceable. I would do anything for my baby sister. And I know she has my back 1,000 percent. Today we're meeting up to exercise the chips on our credit cards.

I see Melissa's white Lexus NX 300 pulling into the mall's parking lot just as I'm pulling my silver Audi S8 into an empty parking space near the front of one of the mall's entrance. I called her cell to let her know there's an empty spot two spaces away from where I'm parked. The moment Mel exited her SUV I felt the bottom half of my face spreading into the hugest smile. You would think It's been years since I've laid eyes on her, but all it takes is about a day for me to start missing her like crazy. We embraced right there in the parking lot like Celie and Nettie after Mister sold Nettie. I kissed her cheek and hugged her neck again. "Hey Sugar! You are looking too cute today! All of this for little old me?"

"I knew you weren't going to step out in these street looking anything less than amazing so you know I had to make sure I was just as cute as you. Didn't need you showing me up today."

"Well, you never know who's looking. Now let's get in this mall and see what we just have to have."

Mel and I entered into the mall through the food court. We always come in through that way because it's usually our last stop before leaving.

"So what's on your agenda tonight? Anything planned with your hubby or your honey?"

"My honey wants to take me to this new poetry spot. The poets are suppose to be some of the hottest in town and I hear the food and drinks are to die for. I'm looking forward to it. What about you? Have anything planned this evening?"

"I think Drew is up to something. He's been sneaking around all day and I heard him on the phone with Mama asking her to babysit the girls for him. He's never as sneaky or incognito as he thinks he is, but I do appreciate all the effort he puts in. So I don't ruin it by trying to uncover the surprise."

"Ok Brother-in-law! I wonder what he has planned."

"Don't act like you don't already know. Whatever it is was probably your handy work."

"I plead the fifth." She was right about me knowing what the surprise is, but I can't take credit for the concept. Not this time. This was all Drew's doing. Although, he did call me to get my input, Drew has gotten a whole lot better at surprising my sister. It's not that he isn't romantic or that he doesn't know what appeases his wife. Melissa is just a hard person to surprise. Always has been. She can't stand not knowing something. If she gets a whiff of a secret or a surprise her spidey senses starts tingling, and she doesn't let up until she figures it out. Which is why I'm having the hardest time believing she's just going to let her husband get away with surprising her tonight. Maybe she's getting soft in her old age.

I absolutely love the scent of the mall. It smells like apples and cotton candy. Green apples and pink cotton candy. If my husband wouldn't mind the house smelling like a bachelorette's pad, I'd clone this fragrance for my home. Walking past Nordstroms, a pair of red Steve Madden high heeled boots caught my eye. I instantly knew the outfit I would wear them with. I grabbed Mel's arm and pulled her into the store. Once inside, I saw a pair of black glitter Christian Louboutins. My heart dropped when I laid eyes on them. I had to have both pair. I am in shoe heaven. I could easily grab three more pair, but I decide to show a little restraint and see what the rest of the mall has to offer. I've been wanting a camouflage jumpsuit, but I don't have the exact style in mind yet. I'll know it when I see it. I'll feel it in my spirit. Hopefully, it jumps out at me today.

"So I was out for my run this morning when I am struck by this massive AHA moment. I realized that me and my honey are, in fact, in a relationship. A relationship that transcends any level of normalcy."

"Well, look who finally decided to come out of denial. I've been telling you that for months now. But your head is hard. You were not trying to hear any of that."

"I know Mel. This isn't the time for I told you so. I'm trying to have a serious conversation with you."

"Ok. You're right. Sorry Sugar. Continue."

"There's no title nor do we play by any specific rules. It's all about the connection we have. It's more of a feeling than a thing. We're not just one thing to each other. We are friends who talk about everything. We're homies who love each other's company and can just hang out doing just about anything. And the sex!"

"Let me guess."

"The sex is amazing!"

"Yep! That was my guess."

"Our sexual chemistry is unmatched. We move in sync when we're together. Like we almost read each other's minds. Like magnets. There's a certain level of trust between us that's just really comforting. We were talking about whatever "this" is last... this morning and even we couldn't put words to it, but we're both in agreement that we don't want it to ever go bad."

"Well, A, you know how I feel about your extramarital activities, but you also know that I care way more about your happiness. And I have no idea how this situation would even play itself out, but you're living in the moment and you're happy and I'm here for it. Besides, anybody that has you lit up like a tree and grinning from ear to ear, I say keep 'em. Hell, life's too short."

"When I think logically about it, I think I should leave this boy alone. I should walk away before anyone gets hurt. And sometimes I actually manage to put a little distance between us. But like boomerangs, we just keep coming back. I had the conversation with him about us not kicking it any more because I need to focus on my husband. He was not happy about that one. It hurt me to hurt him, but I had to do what I had to do. Ultimately, he told me he didn't like it, but he would respect it. A few days later we're talking on the phone and texting like that conversation never happened. That fast, I forgot about all the logic I'd applied to the situation. The next thing I know, I'm in his car with his hand on my thigh."

Mel fell out laughing, "You got it bad!"

"But before his hand touched my thigh he looked at me with a serious face and said 'I really thought you were going to stop messing with me.' I looked back at him and said 'I intended to.' He said, 'I really don't want you to.' So last night, without even thinking, I pushed all logic aside and just allowed myself to feel. It felt completely right. Absolute. Like we were supposed to be there with each other. I laid on his chest. I put my face in where his neck meets his collarbone and inhaled his scent. I held his hands. I stroked his hair. I kissed his cheek. I allowed him to wrap his big ass arms around me and swallow my body in his embrace. I shared my feelings... my thoughts... my music."

"I hate to have to be the one to tell you, Sis, but you're going to have to let this run its course. It's like a virus. There's nothing you can do about it, but let it run its course."

"You know what, Mel, most days I'm ok with that."

Alicia

"Happy birthday, Ma! How does it feel to be the most beautiful 57 year old?"

"Thank you, baby. I feel fantastic. Thankful to see another year."

"I'm thankful for you seeing another year too. I don't know what I would do without you. I love you so much, lady. You have no idea."

"No, I think I have a pretty good idea. And I love you more.

I never understood why people would respond with I love you more after being told I love you. How do you know you love me more? It could be very possible that I just might love you more. Whenever I hear that it always feels like the other person is trying to one-up me. Like our love is somehow a competition and they've taken it upon themselves to deem themselves the winner. I know this is silly. And on a lot of levels I understand the phrase I love you more. I guess it is possible for a person to love another person more. Such as in this case. I love my mother to pieces, but I know the love she has for my sister and I is of no competition. She wins. Hands down. I allow that thought to wash over me before responding,

"Mother knows best. Are you ready for tonight? I can't wait to see you."

"Absolutely! All my babies here at one time, You bet I'm ready! And those grand-babies of mine are growing up so fast that I cant keep up. It seems every time I blink my eyes they've matured another year. Blink, and another milestone has taken place. Before we know it, those girls are going to be driving to away games, walking through college courtyards, and hanging out with boys."

"They are growing up fast. I don't know if it's at light speed, but it sure feels that way."

"Part of me wishes they would stay little forever, but I know that's selfish thinking. I know I have to let them grow and be the people they are destined to be. Look how well that turned out for me the first time."

"Oh! You mean those two girls you raised a while back that grew up to be beautiful, confident and intelligent? I believe one of them is a college professor and the other is a gynecologist. Those girls? I guess they turned out alright."

"Yes, those girls, Mom said through her laughter. They are still my babies."

"Well, maybe they'll stop by tonight for dinner. Who knows?"

"I know! You all better have your butts there. No excuses."

"Way to break character, Ma", I said laughing. "I'll see you tonight. 7 o'clock."

"Ok. See you later, baby."

After hanging up with my Mom I sent a text to my husband to see how he was faring along. I didn't want him to get caught up hanging out with Amir or distracted by work and he misses my mom's dinner. I know he wouldn't intentionally miss it, but Derek does have a way of letting time pass him by sometimes. He gets so wrapped up in things at times that he just loses all sense of time. He replied almost immediately, seemingly reading my mind and the intent behind my text,

Husband: You don't have to worry, I have not forgotten about Mama's dinner tonight. And I have not forgotten to pick up the wine. Sweet red, right?

Me: Yes! Mama loves sweet red wine. Thank you Husband 🤗

****

Derek and I arrived at my mother's house right at 7 o'clock. Mama hates it when we're late. With the wine and flowers in tow, Derek walked around to the passenger side of the car to open my door. After all these years my husband still won't allow me to open my own door or pump my own gas when he's around. Even when he calls himself not speaking to me or when he's annoyed by something I've done, or haven't done. A real gentleman through and through. If I'm being honest, I still love it when he opens my door or pulls out my chair. It's something in those tiny acts that makes a girl feel special and protected. The gesture alone says I got you. I stepped out of the car and made sure my dress was straightened as my husband waited patiently. I grabbed his hand once I was sure my dress was perfect and we walked up to my mother's front door.

I turned the knob and we walked in to an elated greeting from my excited mother. She gave both Derek and I each huge hugs. I love the relationship my husband has with my mom. They're innately close. Derek hands the bouquet of pink roses to my mom, "Happy birthday Mama". My mom gushes as if this was the first time someone has ever given her flowers.

I get excited myself when I see the adorable faces of my nieces, Sydney and Sophia, running down the stairs.

"Auntie! Auntie! Auntie! Uncle Derek! Uncle Derek!"

I think they're more excited to see us than my mother is. How can a person not light up at that kind of enthusiasm. Their vim energy is contagious. I squeeze both girls and kiss their chubby cheeks, "Hello my little munchkins. How are Auntie's babies?" Sydney, a year and a half older than Sophia, says "We're not babies anymore, Auntie."

"Oh my! Pardon me. When did this take place?"

Sophia answered, "When I turned 5 and Sydney turned 6".

Sydney anxiously chimed in, "Yes, but I'm about to turn 7".

"That you are. Well, I'm happy you guys informed Auntie that you're no longer babies, but I'll have you know that you both are going to be my babies forever", I said as I pulled them both in for a hug.

After I let them go, the girls ran over to their Uncle Derek. They each hugged him tight and planted kisses on each of his cheeks simultaneously before racing back up the stairs.

Being surrounded by the people I love most is such a joyous feeling. Although I see them often, it never gets old being around them. I'm never tired of seeing them. I grab the flowers and the bottle of wine we brought and leave Derek to sit and talk with Mama while I run off to look for my amazing sister. I find her in the kitchen filling an ice bucket with ice to chill the wine.

"Hey Sis!", I say smiling ear to ear.

"Hey Sissy!", She screams back. I walk over to her and kiss her on the cheek and hand her the bottle of wine.

"How long have you guys been here?"

"We got here about 30 minutes ago. You know Mama hates it when we're late."

I pull Mom's crystal vase from the cabinet where she stores it and began to fill it with ice water.

"Where's my favorite brothers-in-law?", I ask as I place the roses in the vase and sit them on the counter where Mama can see them.

"Ummm, he's your only brother-in-law."

"I guess, If you want to get technical."

Melissa laughs, "He's upstairs setting up the TV for the girls. You know they can't go five minutes without their Kids YouTube videos."

"Yo! My brother from another mother!", Andrew yells as he's coming down the stairs and spots Derek.

"Speak of the devil."

"But why is he so loud? I don't know who I have to remind more to use their inside voices, Drew or the girls."

"Leave my favorite brother-in-law alone. He's just excited to see his favorite brother-in-law."

"You would think he hadn't seen Derek in months."

"Derek does tend to have that effect on people, present company included."

"Well, he's suppose to have that effect on you. You're married to the man." I turned and poked my tongue out at her as I was leaving the kitchen to go greet my favorite brother-in-law. She laughed.

"Hey Big Head", I said upon entering the living room.

"What up Big Head", Drew said walking over to hug me. In the tightest embrace he picked me up and spun me in circles before placing my feet back on the floor. We've greeted each other that way for as long as I could remember. I adore Drew like the brother I never had. Mel called out from the kitchen asking if we planned to eat dinner while it was still mom's present birthday or were we going to wait for the next one? Mom said, "I guess that's our cue," standing up from the sofa. "We'd better make our way to the table before your sister gets hangry." We all laughed and started walking to the elegantly decorated dining room. Derek rushed over to help Mom from where she was sitting.

Drew called up for the Sydney and Sophia to come downstairs and join us.

Alicia

I'm sitting at my desk in my classroom looking over a few of my student's papers that I have to grade when my phone starts buzzing. Glancing over in its direction I see it's Mama. Immediately, my curiosity rose. Mama never calls me during school hours. This must be important. I sat the papers down and picked the phone up, "Hey Mama. Is everything ok?"

"Hey baby. What makes you think something's wrong? A mother can't just call her child to see how she's doing?"

"Of course, Mama. I'm fine. How are you?"

"I'm great. How's my Derek doing?"

Now I know something's wrong. I feel one of Mama's traps being laid. One, she just saw the both of us last night and two, she talks to Derek almost as much as I do so I have no doubt she knows exactly how her Derek is doing. I take a second to decide whether or not I want to take the bait. I bite, "He's great."

"Does he still make you happy, she asks."

Now I know it's a trap. When we were kids Mama used this tactic to get us to think about whatever we had done wrong. It forced us to see how our actions had effected us and the people around us and what we could have done differently. As teenagers, Mel and I could never see one coming. It wasn't until we were standing knee deep in it when we would finally realize where Mama was leading us. She was the master at that technique. Because of that, at 35, I'm constantly thinking about everything I do from every angle. I know they say curiosity killed the cat, but my inquisitiveness won't let me relax until I know where Mama is trying to lead me.

"Absolutely. Every day, I say as if she she should already know that."

"Then why are you cheating on him?"

A strong gasp escaped my mouth without my permission. What the fuck? How does she know this? The only other person, besides my honey, who knows this is Mel. I know Mel's not out here in these streets snitching. But how does Mama know? Did she spot us out? I don't think so, because that would mean she would have seen us before this weekend and there's no way she would have sat on this all weekend. Especially, since she had all night last night to say something. Did Derek tell her? Does he know? Heat blanketed my entire body. My palms are sweating now. I'm actually speechless.

"I know you heard me lil girl", I heard Mama say.

My mind's racing at the speed of light trying to make sense of what's happening right now. I hear her and I want to respond, but my mouth won't cooperate.

"Huh", I finally managed to say. I know better than to Huh my mother, but it's all I got. Even knowing the usage of the word huh is my mother's pet peeve, it was the only word in my arsenal. If you could huh, you could hear she used to say to my sister and I. I have no doubt it's coming now.

"Don't huh me. If you can..."

"Huh you can hear" I said along with her.

"Well, if you know better do better. Now answer my question. Why are you cheating on him? There's no need to deny it, either, because your response on this phone has confirmed what I already suspected. Now tell me why."

I put my head down, "I didn't mean to, Mama, I swear. It just happened."

"It just happened", she says. "So you mean to tell me you accidentally fell on another man's penis?"

Covered in guilt, shame and embarrassment, not just because of my recent behavior or the fact that Mama is calling me on my shit, but by the word penis coming out of my mother's mouth. I struggle to find my next words.

"Ummm..."

"Save it. There are no amount of words you could string together to justify what you've been doing. You have a good man. A man that would move Heaven and Earth for you and this is the way you show your love? I raised you better than this. There is nothing honorable about your behavior. In here shamelessly smiling and texting some other man while your husband is sitting in the next room. And had the nerve to be blushing, at that", Mama said preposterously. "I don't need you to say anything to deny it either. I've lived long enough to know that only a man can put a grin like the one you wore last night on a woman's face. All I want to hear is you saying you're going to make it right. If it's this other man you want to be with then be honest about it. Try to salvage some of your integrity and tell Derek. Let him go. It's not fair to him. But if Derek is still the man of your dreams, then you best end it with whoever he is. You are grown and I wouldn't normally get involved with what you have going on in your personal life. In fact, I wasn't going to say anything about this, but it was stirring my spirit and I couldn't shake it. Slept on it and woke up with it just as heavy on my mind. I had to speak on it. I love you, unconditionally. You know this. I would never turn my back on you no matter what you do. I love Derek like a son, but you are my child and I want you to be happy. Whatever decision you make would be alright with me, but you have to make this right. You hear me, Alicia? You have to make this right."

"I hear you Mama, and you're right. I've known deep down that this is wrong, but I let my greed and selfishness get the best of me. It all happened so fast. One night of drunken passion took the form of a full blown relationship before I knew what was happening. I love the other guy, but the thought of living without my husband crushes my insides. I'm going to make this right Mama. I'm going to let the other guy go."

"Good. And don't go unloading this on Derek, he doesn't deserve that. I love you, baby, but this is your bed to lie in. Don't make him lay next to you."

"Yes Mama."

"Ok baby. I'll let you get back to work. Talk to you soon. I love you."

"Love you too, Mama. Talk soon."

I don't know what makes her think I could just get back to work after a conversation like that. Only Mama can call and drop a bombshell in the middle of your day and lovingly keep it moving as if nothing happen. I feel sick in the pit of my stomach. I gather the papers I was grading before Mama called and slipped them into my work bag along with my iPad and headed home for the day. Closing my classroom door behind me only one thought ran across my mind. Mama is undefeated. Still laying traps in my adult life.

Derek

Conference calls, meetings, and endless emails have occupied my entire day. I haven't even had a minute to grab something to eat. Amir and I have been working on this case involving one of our clients, a night club and a bottle girl. Sometimes I'm truly over the idiocy of a few of the clients we represent, but it's that same idiocy of the rich fools that affords me my lifestyle so I have to take the good with the bad. Most days I love what I do, but there are moments when I'm mentally exhausted and I'm not prepared to meet the ignoramus on their level. Honestly, you would think a little common sense is all a person would need to avoid some of these situations, but where there's trouble there's an opportunity for a fool to find it.

Amir stuck his head in my office, "What do you say we grab some eats? This case isn't going anywhere and my belly is angry."

"Yeah, mine too. Give me five minutes and I'll meet you at the elevators. I'll let you pick the spot."

"Bet", he said closing the door.

The phone rang, "Mr. Simmons, I have your wife on line one", my assistant Kelsee said.

"Go ahead, send her through."

I didn't even let the phone finish it's first ring before picking the receiver up, "Hello beautiful."

"Hey husband. I haven't heard from you all day. Busy day?"

"Yeah, sorry about that. It's been non-stop since I walked through the door this morning."

"No worries, I figured you were having one of those days and knew you wouldn't stop to eat so I..."

As my wife was speaking, I heard three quick taps on my office door then saw Kelsee stepping in with what looks like take out.

"This was just delivered for you", Kelsee said before sitting the bag on my desk.

"Thank you, Kelsee. And thank you babe", I said into the phone turning my attention back to Alicia.

"I don't know how you do that thing where you just know, but I really appreciate it."

"It's a super power", she retorted through light laughter.

"There's enough grub for you and Amir. If I know anything, I know the two of you are just alike in this instance. Neither of you have paused to eat."

"Thank you so much baby. He just stuck his head in here saying we should go grab something and here you've bought something to us."

"It's my pleasure. Just taking care of my man. I'll let you two get to it while it's still hot. What time do you think you'll be home?"

"I'm not sure, but I can't wait to see you. I miss you, woman."

"I miss you too. I'll see you later. Love you."

"I love you too."

I ended the call and dialed Amir's extension, "Hey Bro, come by my office. We're eating in."

"Oh word? I'm on my way."

Alicia

" I'm sorry for the short notice flight babe. I promise, it's only for one day."

"Babe, don't be silly. You don't have to apologize to me for doing your job."

"I know. I just feel guilty sometimes for always having to work and leaving you alone."

"Listen. We're a team, and we both do what we to do for the team. All I want you to worry about is landing this client and coming back home to me in one piece."

"I love you, woman, you know that."

"Yeah, yeah, yeah. Don't get all mushy on me."
We both laughed.

"I love you too. Be safe and I'll talk to you later."

I ended the call with my husband and got out of my car. I walked to the trunk and gathered my overnight bag and a pair of heels for work tomorrow. I hit the button to set the alarm on my car as I walked up the lighted pathway leading to my honey's front door. Before I turned my key in the door, I could hear Janet Jackson's Twenty Foreplay. I dropped my keys in the glass bowl on the table sitting by the front door. The house smelled of vanilla and lilac. I'm a sucker for a good scent. All of the tension left my body the moment I inhaled the warm vanilla and fresh cut lilac. Hearing Janet moaning throughout the house made my belly tingle with arousal. I came to see my honey because I can't go too long without laying eyes on him. Without touching him. If I didn't know any better I'd say he misses me as much as I've missed him. Tonight was different though. Derek had fly out last minute to meet with a potential client, so for the first time I get to spend the night with my honey. I couldn't let this moment pass without taking full advantage of it. I may never get another one.

I called out for him, but no answer. I figured he didn't hear me over the music. I walked to his bedroom to find candles filling the room with the most alluring scent. Still no sign of my honey. I walked down the hallway that led to the master bedroom. When I walked through the door I noticed there was a small tray of pineapple, grapes and melon on the night stand to the right of his bed. I pulled my shoes off and placed them, along with my overnight bag, in the closet before I walked over to taste a piece of pineapple. Right as the sweet juices of the pineapple hit my tongue, I felt my honey's arms softly wrap around my waist accompanied with his breath on my neck and his voice in my ear saying "Hello beautiful." The intensity of that combination was more than I could handle. My body weakened, as a surge of energy spread through me from my neck to my knees like a tidal wave. Moments like this are what make it impossible for me to leave him alone. I have no control over my own body when he's around. Not even a kiss yet and I could feel the wetness pooling between my thighs. I smiled and leaned into his embrace, "It's been too long".

"You're absolutely right."

I turned around to kiss him. Needed to taste him. We shared a kiss that felt as though we were draining each other of the other's energy. Like we were feeding on one another. I could taste his passion as he gave me his tongue, and he took mine as he sucked my bottom lip. He whispered, "I'm in control tonight."

He unbuttoned my blouse while he stared into my eyes. I could see the intensity burning behind his eyes. He peeled my jeans away from my thighs following the trail with kisses down one leg and his tongue moved up the other. After sliding my jeans over my feet, he stood to look at me. Twirling me around to take in the full view. I felt his strong hand grab a handful of my hair, pull my head back and bite down on my exposed neck. With his other hand on the small of my back guiding me to the bed. He laid me down while kissing me slowly. I could kiss him all night. I didn't want him to stop. He leaned over and grabbed another piece of pineapple and fed it to me. He knew those were my favorite. I laid my head back on the pillow and savored the tangy sweetness. With my eyes closed I felt the cool juice from the fruit drip on my neck then a piece made its way down the side of my neck, over my collarbone, across my left breast, and down the middle of my stomach where it stopped on my belly button. If I had to guess, I'd say it was a piece of melon.

 Suddenly, I felt the warmth of his tongue on my neck. Without my consent, my back arched and a slight moan slipped through my lips. It was as though his tongue, and his body for that matter, was tailor made for my body. The warmth followed the wet path left behind by the fruit. It felt like a soft, warm, silky, sponge that contoured perfectly to the shape of every curve of my body it touched. Once he made it to the fruit, he ate it quickly, and continued until he found my love. He drank my juices. My body quivered at his touch. This was pure ecstasy. He did all the things I like. I could do this all night. He made his way up to my face. Taking in his seductive reaction to this moment we shared made me crave him more. He threw his hand around my throat and squeezed just right; whispering I love you in my ear while simultaneously sliding himself into me brought all of my undivided attention to this moment. Forced me to be present because I did not want to miss the slightest detail.

****

With my head still spinning and from pleasure and slow jams softly playing on the bedroom speakers, I drifted off to sleep wrapped snuggly in my honey's arms. The cherry on top was waking up to him. It was everything I imagined it to be. We showered together. Got dressed and ready for work together. We didn't move around his room as if I were a visitor. We never ended up in each other's way. I never felt like he was invading my space, or I was invading his. We moved between the bedroom, bathroom & closet like it was all too familiar. And if I'm completely honest with myself, it felt pretty damn good.

Alicia

I could have sworn I saw my husband's car drive past me right as I was turning onto my honey's street. He's expecting me, but I refuse to pull into the driveway until I know for sure that wasn't my husband circling the block. Maybe I'm just being paranoid. What reason would Derek have for being in this area of town at this hour? When I spoke to him last, he was stuck at the office. I wonder if I've given him a reason to believe I'm being unfaithful. Haunted by wary nagging at me, I drove around the block and then another and then another in an attempt to ensure I wasn't being followed. I think it's all in my head. I don't know why I allow my imagination to run off and get the best of me at times. I made my way back to my honey's house. Finally pulling into the driveway, I can see the light on in the foyer. I dare not keep my honey waiting any longer. I get out of the car and step around to the trunk to grab my bag. I always keep a bag packed with extra clothes, toiletries, socks, underwear and things of that nature. Just as I like to be ready to get a run in on the fly, I also like to be prepared for a trip to my honey's house. I used my key to let myself in. Honey was sitting on the sofa in a pair of red plaid pajama bottoms and no shirt. Instantly, I wanted to jump into his lap and have my way with him. But I resisted the urge and decided to take a shower first so that I could wash the day off.

"Well, hello sweetness," his deep voice turned me on every time he spoke.

"Hey honey", I said walking over to the sofa where he sat comfortably watching some basketball game or another. I leaned over to kiss him and greet him properly when he sat up and grabbed my face in his hands and kissed me like he'd been waiting all day to do that. It was something about when he grabbed ahold of my face in both hands that melted me from the inside. Something magical that always seemed to make everything right in the world. It's as if he casts a spell that places me under a trance. How does he do that? How does he know just what to say, what to do, how to touch me, when and where to touch me to turn my insides to mush? He has magic powers. Or at least he has that magic power over me and my emotions. Because of his magical power, I had fallen into a long fervent kiss that I had to fight to break away from. It felt like I was fighting to wake myself up from a bad dream. Finally, I was free.

"I'll see you in a few minutes, Mister. Give me a few minutes to get cleaned up."

"Don't be long. I've missed you."

I headed towards the master bedroom to get undressed and slide under the warm waterfall of the shower. I moved around my honey's home with comfort and familiarity. I feel a slight sense of home when I'm here. He has gone out his way to make me feel at home, although we both know this can never truly be my home. We're both aware that my real home is the one I share with my husband. The home that has Mr. and Mrs. Simpson's names on the deed. The home that contains the bed we share. The home where the mail delivered is addressed to Derek and/or Alicia Simpson. But this home. My honey's home. This home that I get to temporarily share with him allows us to momentarily live in denial. This home affords us the ability to live in this world we've created where it's just he and I. This home gives us the freedom to just be us without fear of exposure. So I loved this home almost as much as I loved the home I share with my husband. Even if only for a few stolen moments here and there.

Before getting undressed, I walked over to the stereo to put on some shower music. My honey knows that I can't live without my radio, so he had ceiling speakers installed throughout his home so that I would be able to listen to whatever, whenever, wherever I was in the house. I chose India.Arie Songversation. Track 2 is one of my favorite songs in the world. It always gives me so much energy whenever I hear it. Strong, positive, inspiring energy that makes me feel like I can conquer the world. I decided to listen to this one on repeat while I showered. I turned the volume up loud on the bathroom speakers so that I could sing in the shower and not have to feel self-conscious about my singing voice. Or lack thereof.

I removed my clothes and tossed them into my garment bag to be brought to the cleaners. I tied my locks up into a bun that sat at the top of my head so that it would be out of the way of the falling shower water. I wasn't in the mood for a soggy pillow tonight because I allowed my hair to get wet in the shower. There is nothing sexy about that. I stepped into the shower, turning the nozzle all the way to the left so that the hot water would come raining down on me. After about a minute steam began to invade the bathroom, taking over the space as if it owned the place. The water temperature is nice and hot, just like I like it. I stood under the water letting it wash over my face, then the rest of my body. The hot water relaxed me while India got me excited all over again. It was a weird combination, but it made me feel good. Made me happy. I let the cycle of relaxation and excitement take me away. After the third spin of track 2 I decided I should probably wash off and hop out. I do remember leaving a sexy somebody on the sofa waiting for me. I grabbed my Tahitian mango scented soap and squeezed it onto my towel. I worked up a thick lather and began washing the day away. After washing my feet, I started to rinse the soap from my towel before rinsing it from my body when I felt a cool breeze brush past my back. I heard the shower curtain swish open.

"You just couldn't wait a few more minutes, could you? Well, you're a few minutes too late because I'm just about to hop out."

"No, I think I'm just in time".

Startled, I jumped and spun around incredulously to find my husband standing in my honey's bathroom staring me right in the face wearing a look of disbelief and anger. My heart sank to the bottom of my belly. Speechless, I opened my mouth to speak but nothing came out. He opened his mouth to speak when I heard the soft slow twinkle of my alarm notification. The sound grew louder and louder. I could no longer hear India blasting through bathroom ceiling speakers. I felt the strong hold of my husband's arm wrapped around me, pulling me closer to him when my eyes started to open slowly.

"Aren't you going to get that?", he said groggily.

I reached over to the nightstand that sat on my side of the bed and grabbed my phone. TIME TO GET UP flashed across the top of my screen above the dancing alarm clock. After tapping the icon to silence the gentle song, I laid my head back on my pillow, closed my eyes, took a deep breath and thanked God that it was all a dream.

Derek

I couldn't wait to get back home to my wife. I hate having to sleep without her. Thankfully, this was a quick trip. The other partners and I have been after a huge client who would definitely bring in a lot of money for the firm. She had been sitting on the fence for a couple weeks now, so we decided it would be in our best interest if one of us partners flew in to seal the deal. If I were choosing, I would have sent Amir. I love my brother and all, but he was the only one of us who didn't have a significant other or kids waiting for him to get home. But I didn't get to choose and I drew the short straw. So off I went to DC to gain the trust of and convince Mrs. Smith to finally allow my firm to represent her company. I took her to lunch and laid out my best pitch. By the end of lunch Mrs was signing and initialing next to every X and arrow within the contract. No matter how many times I do this song and dance it never gets old. I enjoy closing a deal now just as much as I did when I first started out as a baby lawyer. It still feels like mini victories.

After lunch all I could think about was getting home to my wife. I went back to the hotel the firm put me in and collected my things. I wasn't due to checkout until tomorrow. Admittedly, San Diego is a beautiful city. The weather is perfect and I'm surrounded by beautiful people. A different kind of man would have enjoyed the extra day with the luxurious hotel suite. Jogged on the beach with it's beige sand and turquoise water, swam with the dolphins, lounged poolside while sipping Mai Tais, slept in the king sized bed covered in 1800 thread count sheets, ordered room service and ate it in that king sized bed. All of that would add up to the perfect vacation to any other man, but without my wife here with me it's all worthless. I packed light for this trip being that it was a quick trip, and I didn't really unpack what little I had once I checked in. This trip for me really was about getting the client to sign the contract. Now that that mission is accomplished, it's time I make my way back home.

****

Once I'm home sweet home all I want to do is shower so that I can wash this trip off of me and relax until my wife gets home. After disarming the alarm I head upstairs to do just that. I take in the scent of my home as I jog up the stairs. There really is no place like home. I undress and toss my clothes into the dry-cleaning hamper. While I wait for the water to get hot in the shower I call Alicia to let her know I've made it back safely. It goes straight to voicemail. That's a little odd. She never turns that thing off, not even when she's running. Maybe her battery died. I leave her a voicemail telling her how much I've missed her and how I can't wait for her to get home, along with a few naughty things I want to do to her once she gets here. Seeing all those couples together in San Diego only made me want to have my wife in my arms even more. Put my mind in a state that had me thinking of ways to make her moan. Ways to make her back arch. Ways to put that look of fire and desire in her eyes.

I step into the shower and let the water rain down on the top of my head and trickle down to the rest of my body. I take note of how quiet my home is. It's not that I'm afraid of being home alone, more like something about this quiet was unfamiliar. No music playing, no TV on, no washer or dryer running downstairs. Nothing. Just the sound of the water running in this shower and me breathing. How is it that I'm able to hear the sound of my own breath? This quiet is almost deafening. After showering, I step out of the walk-in shower and wrap a towel around my waist. Upon walking back into the bedroom I eyed the bed warily. I hadn't noticed when I first got home, but it had been made perfectly. Too perfectly. Almost like I made it myself. Alicia makes our bed because she knows I like for the bed to be made, but if she had her way she'd never make it. She doesn't see the point. So needless to say it's not her favorite thing to do nor has she perfected the tight angles of the military corners. Maybe I'm being a little paranoid. I'm bugging. I'm sure something is nagging at my mind, but I can't really explain it. It's more of a feeling. A gut feeling. I dry off and throw on some black joggers and a grey v-neck t-shirt and head downstairs to the kitchen to make something to eat. I pore myself a glass of bourbon. Hopefully, it'll calm my mind so I can relax a little.

Alicia

Since my talk with Mama I've been extremely torn. I know she's right and I should walk away from this mess I've made, but it's much easier said than done. I've tried. I've been trying. I've known in my heart of hearts that what I'm doing is wrong and that my husband doesn't deserve this. I want to do right by him and the vows I took, but my honey has a hold so strong on me that I have yet to master how to get out of. I can't escape his touch. His smell. The way he kisses me and I lose control of my legs. The way he wraps me up in his arms. The way he peers through me with those beautiful brown eyes I swear he can see my soul. It's like I've been sucked into a vortex I can't break free of. A very pleasurable vortex, but a forbidden vortex, nonetheless. At this point, it would hurt me to walk away from my honey, but it would hurt me more if my husband walked away from me. How did I allow this to happen? Why have I given another man permission to know me, to touch me the way that is supposed to be reserved for my husband? Normally, this would not be weighing so heavy on my heart. I would be able to enjoy the vortex without a second thought of the consequences, but ever since my mom called me out on it things haven't been the same. I spent an entire night with this man, something I never saw me doing, and the whirlwind was amazing, don't get me wrong. However, the moment I entered my car the gravity of it all hit me all at once. I really am a piece of shit. Or at least I feel like one.

Derek

I've been so busy working on this case that I haven't had a chance to spend any real quality time with my wife in quite some time. I barely get to see her these days. Most mornings she's up and out of the door for her morning run before I'm up for work, and I'm working late at the office most nights which means Alicia's already in bed by the time I make it in. I'm grateful that my wife is as driven as I am, so she understands when we go through these periods of scarce interaction. But tonight I'm shutting work down early and I'm carving out some time for her. Just because she understands doesn't make it okay to take advantage of it or overdo it. So tonight is her night. My wife works so hard, and she's so invested in those kids she deserves someone to be fully invested in her as well. I know I'm not always around, but when I am here I need my wife to feel as exceptional as she is.

After considering a few five star hotels that my wife has not spent the night in, I decided to make a reservation at the W hotel. I planned this evening with my wife in mind. I want to nail all of her favorite things so I know for sure she'll enjoy herself. Tonight isn't about me at all. I've consulted with my little sister, Mel, at just about every turn. Although I know what makes my wife smile, it never hurts to get a second opinion from the only other person that knows her as well as I do. I just want to make sure I cover all of my bases and nothing is forgotten. I want to wow her. She deserves it. I don't want tonight to resemble anything we've done in the past. I reached out to the hotel about their spa when, midway through the conversation, the thought hit me. It would be much more enjoyable for the both of us if I play masseuse tonight. I just need to get my hands on a massage table to give her that real spa-like experience. I'm so excited, I cannot wait to see the look on Alicia's face when she sees what I've put together for her. I still have to make a few more stops before I make my way to the hotel to set everything up, but first I'd better call my wife so that she doesn't make any other plans.

Alicia

Laying in this lavender scented room with this man's hands on my body is everything I need right now. Lord knows I love this man. I was at my desk, grading papers, when I got the unexpected phone call to meet him at the W hotel for 7 p.m. He told me all I needed to pack was my sexy sun kissed body and a smile. I can definitely do that. I didn't even question it. I was instantly excited by the consideration. I really appreciate him. After all these years, he's still so thoughtful. Even through all the chaos life throws our way, my husband always finds the time for us to connect. I know sometimes it's not easy, and downright impossible other times, but Derek constantly tries to make time for us. How can you argue with a man like that? So when he said to leave everything and meet him at the W, that's exactly what I did. No questions asked. He could have told me to meet him in the middle of the Conga, and I would have. Because I know wherever he is is where I want to be. And wherever we are is bound to be special.

When I arrived I walked over to the front desk, told them my name and that I was looking for Derek

Simpson. The receptionist asked to see my ID. I dug through my bag until I found my wallet holding my driver's license and all of my credit cards and handed it to her. She smiled when she returned it to me, showing off a gorgeous dimple in her right cheek. I admired her dimple as she typed quickly on her computer's keyboard. Finding the information she needed, she reached inside of her desk drawer and retrieved a plastic hotel room key. As she did some more typing, she asked if I needed any assistance with my bags. When I told her I didn't pack anything, she glanced up at me with a smirk that I could tell was there to hide the full on grin she really wanted to have.

"Here you are, Mrs. Simpson." Pointing to her left, "The elevators are just around that corner. You're going to go up to room 521. Enjoy your evening and don't hesitate to let us know if it's anything we can do to make your stay here more pleasurable."

I smiled at the receptionist wearing the beautiful dimple, "Thank you so much. You enjoy the rest of your day. And I'm sure everything will be to my liking."

Walking through the hotel's first floor to the elevators, I took in the ambiance. This really is an exquisite hotel. Once I stepped onto the elevator, I was

ENTANGLED

giddy with excitement. I could not wait to see what my man has planned for us.

I exited the elevator and walked down the marble tiled hallway until I reached room 521. I slipped into the card into the key slot and walked into Paradise. He would pop for the suite. This man doesn't do anything small. He lives by the go big or go home motto. I heard Silk playing just loud enough to drown out any noises that may be coming from this room once I get my hands on this chocolate man of mine. He knows this is my song, and every time I heard it I just wanted to lay with him. The room was lit by candlelight. There was a trail of silver wrapper Hershey's Kisses and white rose petals starting from the door headed down a short hallway. I hung my purse on the coat rack next to the door and followed the trail. A few steps in, there was plain pink card lying amidst the the petals and Kisses. I stooped down to pick it up.

Girl you for me
And girl me for you
I don't care what people might say
Just ask and I'll do
I'll do it for you
There'll be no more games that we play

-Silk

The lyrics to the Silk song playing. Now I'm getting all emotional. I know this isn't the time for it, but it melts my heart seeing all the effort my baby put into this evening. Fighting back happy tears, I continue to follow the trail down the short hallway. Entering into the main room, my breath is completely taken away taking in the astonishing beauty of this room. Candles everywhere. A huge king sized bed with plush turquoise and white bedding. As I walked a little closer, I noticed there were gold wrapper Kisses on the bed that spelled out I LOVE YOU; accompanied by red rose petals. Absorbing the atmosphere of this breathtaking suite, I scanned the room searching for that sexy husband of mine so that I can wrap my arms around his neck and kiss him desirously. The trail of Kisses and petals stopped at the large bed, but another plain pink card was among the red rose petals.

Now is the time to relax your mind
Let go and unwind
I've waited far too long, I'm ready
Tonight's the night for loving you right
You know what I wanna do

Wanna give it to you baby
-Brandy

More lyrics. Another one of my favorites. Suddenly, I felt the presence of the man I've been yearning for since my afternoon phone call telling me when and where to show up this evening. He was standing behind me with his arms around my waist.

"Hello Mrs. Simpson."

10 years of marriage and I still loved to hear him refer to me as his Mrs. He slid my locks to one side, and kissed me softly on the other side of my neck.

"Oh my God! Why would you do that!", I laughed as I tried to squirm out of his hold. He knew that was the one thing I could not take. A kiss on the neck. It possessed the perfect blind of turning me on and tickling the shit out of me all at the same time. He found it funny that a grown woman could be so ticklish, yet it excited him to know he was also creating moisture in my panties. Once I stopped trying to fight against his grip, he whispered in my ear, "I have missed you something serious, woman."

Turning to face him, I looked up into his eyes, "Thank you so much, baby. I really appreciate you." I kissed him like I hadn't laid eyes on him in months. Like I wouldn't see him for months.

"I love you too, Mrs. Simpson", he said knowing exactly what I meant behind that kiss.

"I love you more."

He kissed my lips again then slowly reached for my hand. He took my hand and walked me toward what looked like a dark room from where we stood. When we got a little closer I realized it was the opening to a massive bathroom. More red and white petals. More Kisses. My husband stopped and turned to me, staring at me for a second. He began to unbutton my blouse before he slid it off of my shoulders and let it hit the floor. I admired the way he took his time undressing my carefully. My husband then unfastened my skirt and slid it to the floor while his hands rubbed my legs on the way down. He laughed a little when he saw I wasn't wearing any panties. Once he reached my ankles, he one by one removed my heels. Sitting them off to the side. He leaned in and kissed my right thigh. His soft lips feeling like silk and marshmallows against my skin. It kind of tickled, but I resisted the urge to squirm. I loved this man and the way he makes me feel. Every day with him feels like the beginning. We still have that new car smell even after all these years. He kissed my thighs until he got to my belly, where he stopped to swirl his tongue in small circles. I stood there enjoying the moment with my eyes closed and my head leaned back. When the kisses stopped I opened my eyes to look down at him. He was standing.

"Why did you stop?"

"Because now is not the time."

Once again, he grabbed my hand and we walked over to this gigantic jacuzzi tub the size of an outdoor hot tub. It was filled with bubbles and petals. Candles with the scent of vanilla and lavender surrounded the tub. It all looked so inviting.

"I can't believe you did all of this for me, babe."

"You hush. You deserve this."

"Are you going to join me? There's more than enough room for the both of us."

"Do you want me to join you?"

"You already know I do."

"You wish I my command."

I kissed my husband on his cheek and smiled. I looked him his eyes wearing a smirk as I pulled his polo across his stomach and chest, then over his head. I kissed him again on the lips as I unbuckled his belt and pants. I bent over slowly to pull his pants and briefs to the floor. He moved to pull his feet out of his pants when I tapped his foot, "I got this."

He placed his foot back on the floor, throwing his hands up in renunciation, "Ok, Mrs. Simpson, whatever you say."

I pulled the pants and briefs from around his feet. As I went to stand I caught a glimpse of one of my favorite parts of him. I call him Lil Derek. Although, there's nothing little about him. I couldn't help but to kiss Lil Derek on his head like Big Derek had kissed my thigh. I was just returning the favor. I stood up in front of my husband admiring all the hard work he puts in in the gym. I thought to myself, I am such a lucky woman. I grabbed ahold of his hand and took him over to the tub. We passed in front of the tub. My husband walked behind me and began to pull my locks up into a bun that sat on the top of my head. I giggled a little. He knows me so well.

"So you've just thought of everything, haven't you?"

He kissed the back of my neck, "I knew you wouldn't get in that water with your hair down. So yeah, I came prepared."

I shied a little under the ticklish sensation, "I see!"

ENTANGLED

There was a table-like area attached to the tub where my husband had two glasses of my favorite wine sitting. There was also a small bowl of strawberries. I held on to my husband's chest as I climbed into the water. The water was nice and hot just as I like it. He would say it's too hot. I can tell now that it wasn't a part of the plan for him to get in with me. I smirked at that realization.

Before I sat down, I spotted another note folded next to the bowl of strawberries. I sat in the warm water and unfolded the red card, while my husband climbed in.

I want to give you my life
my strength
my will to be here
That's the least I can do
Let me cater to you
Through the good
The bad
The ups and the downs
I'll still be here for you
Let me cater to you
'Cause you're beautiful
I love the way you are
Fulfill your every desire
Your wish is my command...

-Destiny's Child

"So you're going to fulfill my every desire?"

I felt his hand sliding slightly between my lower lips, "Every single one."

I purred at his touch. I leaned back and rested my head on the back of the tub while my husband stirred my honey pot. I enjoyed the attention. My eyes slowly closed as I became more and more aroused by his touch. He came a little closer to me. Just close enough for him to plant soft kisses on my breasts. One. Then the other. He chose one to lick. Slow circles around my nipples, then a soft suction on my nipple. The combination of attention he showed my nipples and honey pot was almost too much to bare. I wanted him right there in the tub. I leaned in and kissed him, "I love you."

"I love you too", he said in the sexiest voice I've ever heard him use. I think that turned me on more than the kissing and sucking. We sipped our wine and continued our foreplay until we were both almost wrinkle.

"I think we should be getting out now. We're starting to wrinkle up, and ain't nothing sexy about that."

"To this day, I do not understand how a man who's been to college and law school, prepare legal briefs just about every day, and argue serious cases in front of judges manages to find the word ain't in his vocabulary."

He laughed, "Easy. It's in the dictionary."

I almost scowled at his sarcasm, "Let's just get out, silly. The water is getting cold."

****

Now I'm laying on this massage table with my husband's hands covered in oil moving up and down the back of my legs. This feels so good, complete Heaven. The hotel has a spa that offers massages, but my baby said he was going to be the only person touching my body tonight. So he ordered a massage table especially for tonight. I don't deserve this man. I don't know how I became so lucky. This night couldn't get any better. Once my husband finished massaging my feet, he planted a series off soft kisses down my back. I can't wait to get up off of this table and into the bed. Then it's going to be my turn to cater to him. After a few more kisses on my back led him back up towards my neck, my husband licked the lobe of my right ear and whispered, "Follow me."

Alicia

Dizzy from ecstasy, swirls of bright oranges and deep reds flashed through the room. I could no longer tell which way was the ceiling and which way was the floor. I could feel my breaths becoming more and more shallow. Light headed, I moaned out from deep pleasure. In the midst of trying to catch my breath I heard a loud crash coming from the front of the house. The sound resembling a car crash. Startled, me and the beautiful man on top of me brought our love-making to a halt. We stared at each other trying to decipher if we each heard the same thing. It was obvious that we both heard the boisterous boom from the other room. A wave of panic and fear ran through my chest to the pit of my belly. Not able to move at first, I watched as my honey leaped out of bed and reached for his clothes. He ran out of the room with extreme urgency. Darted towards the crash. I know this is probably the worst possible time, but it is something very sexy seeing this man jump into action like this. Not really knowing what to do, I also jumped up to fish for my clothes. I could hear yelling from the front of the house as I slipped into my jeans.

"What the fuck do you think you're doing?"

"Me? What the fuck do you do think you're doing?"

"You break into my house in the middle of the night and you want to know what I think I'm doing?"

I recognized the second voice. In complete disbelief, I pulled my tank top over my head as I ran towards the argument. Once I got to the living room, my worst fear had been confirmed. Derek stood in the middle of the living room with his face consumed by rage and hate. I had never seen him look so devilish before. He turned and looked at me as I entered the room. His face moving from rage to shock, then sheer pain. The look on his face shattering my heart.

"What are you doing here?" I know that wasn't an ideal question, seeing that my husband is standing in my honey's living room in front of my honey as I come running from the bedroom. But I was caught completely off guard. But I mean... What was he doing here? How did he know I was here? He's suppose to be at the office. Why wasn't he at the office? Did he have his investigator follow me? Why was this happening? This isn't happening. It can't be. I glanced at my honey as I did when we first heard the crash. Searching his face for signs of confirmation. Any little signal that this was not really happening right now. His face is covered in uncertainty. Not sure whether he should be concerned for me or prepared to defend himself. I turned my attention towards the front door. I noticed the door frame was broken and the door was wide open. None of this is making any sense to me. I've never known Derek to even have a fist fight in his adult life, let alone crash through the front door of someone's home by force.

"What am I doing here? What the fuck are you doing here? You're supposed to be at the movie theater with Melissa. So why is it that you're running from another man's bedroom with your clothes ineptly thrown on? I love you! I'm good to you. And this is how my love is reciprocated? I wish I'd known I was married to a lying cheating bitch, I wouldn't have wasted all these years on your trifling ass."

"Say bruh! You want to watch your mouth talking to my girl?"

"Fuck you boy! I'm talking to my wife!"

"Fuck you! You're in my house disrespecting my..."

My honey hadn't been able to complete his sentence. Derek flew across the space between them and before I finish blinking my eyes his fist had met the face of my beau after school style. Derek was on top of the man I was making love to just a few minutes ago slamming his fists into his face repeatedly. That beautiful face, now my husband's punching bag.

I stood in place stunned by what has gotten into Derek. My mind trying to make sense of this chaotic moment. It's all happening too fast. I saw my honey switch into fight mode and start to defend himself. Throwing several fierce punches to my husband's ribs allowed him to get Derek off of him long enough for him to get to his feet. Derek rolled over in pain. I don't know whether to console my husband or run to my honey's aid. I watched my honey hold his hand up to his mouth then wince in agony at the touch of his open flesh. Derek got up from the floor. Completely out of character, Derek was a bull and this situation was the red rag being dangled in front of him. He was livid. Deranged. I could tell my honey did not want to fight Derek, but he could see that this is not going to end peacefully. Derek began to scream obscenities at the both of us. I became an ungrateful bitch who he wouldn't piss on if I were on fire. My honey, the punk ass bitch who's ass he was going to whip. In the next second, Derek had his hands around my honey's neck. Ready for the fight, my honey punched Derek in his face.

Before I knew it, the brawl resembled the Looney Tunes fights where all you saw was a big ball of moving dust with limbs flailing from it. Horrified, I don't know whether to try and stop it or dial 911 or wait for them to wear themselves out or what. The way these two are carrying on, like two vicious pit-bulls, I know better than to get in the middle of this melee. I am surprised that none of the neighbors have called the police though. Glancing around the once refined living room, I witnessed absolute turmoil. Just about none of the furniture was standing up right. The sofa was damn near in the dining room. Cushions and pillows scattered across the floor. What use to be a glass bowl, candle holders and picture frames accompanied the cushions and pillows. It wasn't long before the Looney Tunes brawl made its way to the television stand crashing into the 75 inch TV along with the custom made glass stand it sat on.

I couldn't tell who was who any more, until my honey threw my husband into the last piece of upright furniture. A beautiful bookshelf that was home to many extraordinary works? Exhausted, my honey took that moment to catch his breath. My heart immediately sank into the pit of my belly as I was suddenly consumed with fear, grief and disbelief. Before either of us had a chance to react, my husband was barging towards my honey with one of the metal bookends from the bookcase. Derek slammed the metal figure of a man reading a book into the back of my honey's head. It was the most horrific thing I'd ever witnessed.

I gasped. It was the only thing my body would allow to come out of my mouth. I stared at the man I'd been in denial about loving for months lying lifeless on the floor amidst broken glass and fragments of pieces that used to decorate his walls. Horrified, I yelled his name. Seconds later, out of my peripheral, I saw something I could have never imagined I'd ever see. The man I'd loved since college coming towards me with the devil in his eyes and the metal man reading a book in his hand. He raised the metal man over his head and grunted, "Bitch!" Heartbroken, I closed my eyes and prepared for the metal man reading a book to come crashing down on my head...

I was jolted awake from the nightmare. My sudden jerking subsequently jarred my husband awake. "What's wrong, babe? Are you ok?"

"Yeah, I just had a bad dream."

"That must've been some dream to scare you like that."

"It just felt way too realistic."

ENTANGLED

"You want to talk about it?"

"No, it's over now", I said lying back down. Once my head hit the pillow I felt husbands arms wrap around my body. I jumped a little, still a little rattled from the nightmare. Not quite fully being able to determine real life from the dream.

"You sure you ok?"

"Yes. Let's just go back to bed". Lying there in my husbands protective embrace I relaxed. Became comfortable. This familiar feeling brought me back to reality. This man could never hurt me. He has loved me for 15 years. I know he loves me with all he has. Unconditionally. And I love him. So why do I continue with this affair that I know with every fiber of my being would kill him if he ever found out? Why can't I just walk away from what I know in my heart is wrong? Forget about that others guy and just be with my husband the way we both intended when we said our vows. Why? Am I so greedy that it's not enough to have one man that would go to the ends of the Earth to not only be with me but make me happy, but two men who adore the ground I walk on? What are you doing, Alicia? You have got to make some changes. It's not fair to either of these men, but especially not your unsuspecting husband. He doesn't deserve this.

I grabbed ahold of my husband's hand and brought it to my mouth. I kissed the back of his hand and held it there as if I were telling him how sorry I am through this gesture. I whispered softly, I'll do better.

Alicia

"I don't think we should do this anymore."

"What do you mean, Alicia? I love you."

"I love you too." I can't believe I just said that, "But this isn't fair to my husband or you. This isn't how I imagined my marriage going."

He peered at me with those sexy brown eyes; I thought he could see through to my soul. I thought he was able to see what my body was actually feeling. How even in this very moment that I am trying to sever all connections to this man, all my body wanted to do was hold on to him. I wanted to grab him and squeeze him tight. If I'm being completely honest with myself, I actually do love this man. For the longest I didn't want to admit it, but watching him as his heart is breaking before me I can no longer deny how I feel and me actually breaking up with him is beginning to be more than I can handle. I never imagined that when this day finally came just how difficult not only me having to go through it, but also watching as he absorbed my words. Knowing that I am the cause of the pain in his heart shatters my mine. I knew he wouldn't be thrilled about this, but I at least thought that like me, somewhere deep within him he knew we couldn't go on forever. I never led him to believe that I would ever leave Derek. He had to know this affair needed to end eventually. Looking in his eyes now tells me he chose to ignore this fact. He made the decision to turn a blind eye and not acknowledge the notion of us ultimately walking away from this affair.

"Alicia, I need you."

"I need my husband more."

"What about us?"

"It pains me to have to do this, but I think we should let this go before either of us become any more invested."

"My heart is already invested. You are all I think about. All I ever want to do is be with you. I know our situation isn't ideal, but I'm not ready to let you go. I'm not fond of the idea of having to share you, knowing every night you're lying next to someone else. But if that's what I have to do to be with you then that's what I'll do. If stealing a few moments to be near you is what I have to do then that's just what has to happen."

"I don't want to hurt you. I care very much for you. I just don't see how us continuing is going to end well for any of us."

Without another word, he kissed me. He kissed me like it was the last thing he would ever do. My mind told me to pull away, but my body betrayed me. My body could not resist his touch no matter how hard I tried. No matter how loudly my mind screamed GET OUT OF HERE, my body surrendered to his kiss. My mind raced. My knees weakened. My skin heated. I wish I were able to exercise a bit more restraint when it comes to him.

I was finally able to pry myself away from his magnetic pull, "We have to walk away. We can't keep doing this. I know you think that this is what you want, but where would this part-time relationship leave you in 10, 15 years? You can't see it now, but this is for the best."

"I don't like this. Nor do I want to think about 10, 15 years from now. All we have is right now, and right now I want you and only you."

"But I am taken. I'm not available for you to have. I belong to someone else, and this isn't fair to him. As much as it hurts me to hurt you, it would destroy me to hurt him. I often think about our first kiss and how if only I had had the strength to turn away then we wouldn't be here now. But we are, and no amount of reflecting is going to change that. This is where we are. I don't like it anymore than you do."

The man with the hypnotic trance didn't say a word. He just stared at me in deep contemplation.

"I understand where you're coming from. I don't like it. But I understand it. If this is really what you want, I'll respect your wishes and let this go."

The other man I love took my face in his palms and softly kissed my forehead. I felt a tear fall down my cheek. I backed away turned around and walked toward his front door. I removed his house key from my keyring and sat it in the glass bowl on the table next to the front door. I picked up my purse and walked out to my car. It killed me not to look back at him just once more, but I know it would have just made this harder to do had I turned and saw him looking at me with heartbreak in is eyes. So I kept my eyes forward and walked as fast as I could to my car. Once inside, I cried like a newborn. This hurts more than I anticipated. I knew I was developing feelings for him, but I hadn't realized just how serious things had gotten. I cried my last cry. I cried enough for the both of us. I cried until I had nothing left, "Okay, Alicia, pull yourself together, fix your face and get home to your husband.

Alicia

I didn't expect my heart to ache the way it does. I figured I would experience a bit of an adjustment, but this hurts. Hurts for real. Hurts like hell. I keep trying to convince myself that I've made the right decision. Logically, I know I have, but emotionally I'm second guessing all of my decisions that have led me here. Part of me wishes I could go back to the beginning and refute that first kiss. The kiss that kicked off this sex driven emotional whirlwind that sucked me in and refused to let me go. I can let it burn and move on from this though. I'm more than capable of walking away from that situation and being perfectly happy with my husband. I mean, there was life before my honey. Derek made me blissfully happy before the kiss. Surely, we can go back. Right? Only now I feel as though a piece of me is missing. I feel like a part of my heart has been ripped out. I'm lightweight dying on the inside. Where did these feelings even come from? When did they have the audacity to evolve from a meaningless fling into something that possesses the wherewithal to hurt me like this? Maybe I should call him. No I definitely shouldn't do that. A clean break is best. But one little text won't hurt. Will it? I just need the tiniest minuscular piece of him. Then I could wean myself off of his allure for good. That's crazy talk. I have no business reaching out to him at all. I should have never let it get this far. But now that it has, I have to slip into my big girl panties and woman up. We both knew that situation was temporary. I'm a married woman with zero intent on leaving my husband. How far could this thing really have gone? I just didn't expect it to feel like an actual breakup when one of us finally called it quits. He should be free to meet other people. I've been incredibly selfish and remiss with the both of these men. I have a responsibility to my husband to be the woman he married. The woman he believes me to be. And I owe it to my honey to release him so that he may find a love that's all his. My honey. Not anymore. That's going to be a tough one to shake. I'd grown so comfortable referring to him as such. It's become second nature. Even after our demise it just rolls off of my tongue so effortless. What do I call him now? Nothing. Because I'll never see or talk to him again. My ambivalence is driving me crazy. I can't tell if I'm coming or going. My sister is truly a Godsend. I don't know if she sensed I needed a pick-me-up or what, but she certainly came through just when I needed her.

Mel: We're going out tonight. Be ready for 9.

Me: Yes ma'am

I'm so used to Mel's bossy ways, it doesn't even bother me. And honestly, I'm so tired of crying and feeling melancholy that I welcome her and all of her dictatorialness today of all days. It's been two weeks since I broke off my relationship. Two weeks since I've felt his lips on mine. Two weeks since he's held me. Two weeks since I've held him. Two weeks since I've heard his sexy voice in my ear during our conversations on my way home from work. Two weeks since our bodies touched. This has been the longest two weeks of my life. It's weird to be in so much pain and not being able to talk to my husband about it. He's always been peace. My sanctuary. My center. There's no way for him to help me with this though. No way for him to ease the pain in my heart. Although, having him swallow me up in his arms right before my body gives way to sleep has been comforting. Those brief moments I lay in the arms of the man who has loved me unconditionally since before I knew what unconditional love was does offer a certain level of tranquility I so desperately need. But then morning snacks me across the face and I have to go about my day as if everything is business as usual. I could really use the distraction my sister is imposing on me.

Husband: Good afternoon beautiful

Me: Good afternoon husband
Husband: I hope you're having the most amazing day. Just wanted to let you know I'm thinking of you and it looks like it's going to be a long night here at the office.

Me: It's OK babe. Mel has something planned for us tonight. She texted me a little while ago and told me to be ready for 9

Husband: Great. What are you girls getting into?

Me: I have no idea. I didn't even feel the need to question what's on the agenda. You know how Mel is. Once she has her mind made up, it's best to just go with it.

Husband: Yep. Our despotic little Mel. What are you going to do?

Me: Be ready for 9!

Husband: LOL! Exactly!

Husband: OK sweetheart, I'll see you later tonight then.

Me: I look forward to it 😏

Dressed in a short black dress that hugs my well toned body perfectly, my locks in a curly up-down do with a pair of big silver hoop earrings and the black crystal Louboutins I purchased the last time Mel and I went shopping, I slid into my Audi and headed to Mel's house. The best of Luther Vandross playing softly through my car speakers while my mind drifted with thoughts of my honey's hands squeezing my butt after pulling me in for a hug and kiss that says he's missed me. My thoughts teeter on visions of me pulling his shirt over his head so that I could feel the his sculpted body against mine. Needed to feel the warmth of his skin on mine. Wanted to feel his hand in my hair as our tongues danced the dance of a passionate salsa. Before I knew it I was pulling up in my sister's driveway. I was snapped out of my daydream by my phone ringing. I told my car to answer the call. Before I could get Hello out of my mouth, Mel was already yelling through my car's speakers "Where are you?"

"I'm just pulling up. I'm in your driveway."

"Ok, I thought I was going to have to come literally drag you out of your funk."

"No ma'am. Now bring your butt out that house and come on"

"Coming."

We ended the call. A minute later my little sister exited through her front door also wearing a black dress and silver hoop earrings, only her perfect curls hung down her back. Our telepathy at work again. I stepped out of my car to hop into hers, "Great minds really do think alike", Mel said greeting me with our usual hug.

"That's what they say."

I opened the passenger door and carefully climbed into Mel's car, "You want to let me in on where we're going now?"

"We're going listen to some music. A friend of mine has a show tonight. She's really dope. You're going to love her."

****

I could hear the live band before we stepped foot into the club. To step inside and feel the vibration of the band was jolting. My entire core screamed that tonight is going to be epic. My sister grabbed us a table while I headed over to the bar to grab us some drinks. I plan to get white girl wasted tonight. I plan to drink until I can't see and dance until I can't stand. I'm going to drink and dance the hurt away. I make my way back to the table and sit Mel's rum and pineapple juice in front of her while I took my seat across from her and took a sip of my tequila and pineapple juice. I turned my attention to the singer on the club's stage accompanied by the sickest drummer, keyboardist and bass player I've heard in a while. There is something amazing that happens when I hear live music; coupled with the sultry voice of the singer, the perfect cocktail was created. The singer covered the best of the best R&B. She pulled us in with her versions of everything from Deniece Williams's Cause You Love Me, Baby to Jazmine Sullivan's Excuse Me. Excuse Me being my weakness, I fought to control the tornado whirring through my chest and belly. My insides going crazy with excitement. The singer performed as if she was born for this moment right here, and the band didn't miss a beat. Where she went they followed like magnets. After a couple more drinks, Mel and I were on the dance floor cutting up. If I didn't know any better, Mel may have needed to get out just as much as I did tonight. The unexpected turn of events I hadn't planned for was Mel exceeding her three drink limit. My plans of cutting loose were deterred when I became the designated driver. How did this happen? You see where my tolerance surpassed Mel's by a country mile, Mel could not have more than three drinks when we're out because she transforms into an alter ego. Her drunken alter ego is the direct opposite of sober Mel. A lot of fun to be around, but unpredictable, nonetheless. It's because of this that I have to keep a clear enough head to keep us both safe. We both laughed, danced and drank like we had been locked under lock and key all of our lives and tonight was our first night of freedom. By the end of the night we were exhausted and well entertained. I held up my end of the deal and got us home safely. I had Drunk Mel to amuse me on the ride back to her house. Once we pulled into her driveway we exited the car and I walked my baby sister to her door. Right as I was preparing to insert her key into the front door, I heard someone on the other side moving the lock. The door swung open and my brother in law was standing on the other side. One glance at Mel an a look of realization came across his face.

"I take it you ladies had fun."

"A plethora"

"Come on, let's get you to bed", he said swooping his wife up as if he were carrying her over the threshold.

"Thank you for making sure she came back to me in one piece. Are you okay to drive home?"

"Come on now." I said handing him Mel's keys

"You're right. What was I thinking? Call me when you make it in."

"Will do. Make sure she gets some Ibuprofen and water in her." I said walking down the driveway towards my car.

"Will do."

Slightly intoxicated, the ride home only provide time and space for me to think about all the things I wanted to do to my husband once I was in his presence again. The tequila gave my vagina a mind of her own and right now all she could think about is taking in all ten inches of my husband's length. Excited to see Derek's car in the garage, I pulled my heels off and jogged to my door. Once inside, I set the alarm and sent Drew a text

Me: Hey brudda, I'm home safe. Good night.

Brudda: Ok. Don't forget your Ibuprofen and water. Good night big head.

Who did he think he was talking to? I had my Ibuprofen before I left the house. I had learned the preventive measure back in college. Better safe than sorry. Louboutins tucked under my left arm, I hiked my dress up a little to give my legs the room they needed to trot up the stairs two at a time. Once I made it to my bedroom, I pulled the dress off. Anxious and tipsy, I didn't even bother to put it away. I undressed from my bra and left it on the floor next to the dress. With no underwear in my way I ran to the bathroom to wash the club off of me. I emptied my bladder then hopped in the shower for a quick bath. After freshening up I grabbed a big towel that hung from the hook on the back of the bathroom door. I dried my body off, but didn't bother worrying with pesky pajamas. I slipped under the covers and snuggled up real close to my husband. I wrapped an arm around his waist and buried my face in his neck. I inhaled his scent before softly biting him. I ran my hand across his hard belly and found my way past the elastic of his boxer briefs. I stroked him awake as I kissed, licked and bit his neck and back. He let out a soft moan, turned over and said, "Welcome home beautiful," before reciprocating my kisses. His moans rapidly turning me on, mixed with the alcohol running through my system is making me aggressive. It's like a switch is flipped and a dominating spirit envelopes me. I broke away from his kiss and mounted his face. He loves when I take control in this manner, so he happily acquiesced. My husband licked the syrup that had already began to puddle. My back curved backwards and I bit down on my bottom lip smothering a painful sounding whine. He gave me his tongue until I saw fireworks. Twice. After my second explosion I slid down my husband's chocolate body until our bodies were aligned. I grabbed him by the throat and squeezed, kissed him fervently. I sucked and bit his bottom lip as I slid down the length of him. That first stroke causing slight tremors to flood my body. The room now filled with sex sounds. I choked and kissed, rose and fell until my husband's breathing became erratic. His moans louder. His body convulsed uncontrollably. His moans and my seesawing caused my body to erupt in convulsions of its own. The both of our body's going limp with my body collapsing on top of his. We drifted off into La La Land with his deflated erection still inside of me.

Derek

I can't quite put a finger on it, but I can feel a shift in my wife's energy. She's definitely moving differently lately. She appears saddened by something, but she won't say what. I hate seeing her like this and not being able to help her feel better, let alone what's even bothering her in the first place. I'm used to us having fluid communication. We talk to each other about everything, and I mean everything. So for her to hide whatever this is she's going through from me makes me feel less than. Like we're no longer partners. I know it sounds a bit selfish, but it hurts and slightly angers me that she's shutting me out. It's never been a question for as long as we've been us that we are each other's anchors, but watching her drift out to sea without even attempting to let me save her or try and save herself, for that matter, worries my soul. I'm not sure if I should be giving her space to process this on her own terms or if I should push my way in to console her. I kind of feel like the latter would be selfish on my part, but I'm at a loss here. I'm tip toeing in eggshells around the one person I've never had to tip to around before. We've been taking care of each other for what feels like all of our lives, so I don't know how to be with this. I don't know what position I am to play in all of this. The one thing I'm grateful for is she doesn't seem to be pulling away from me. She still snuggles up in the crevice I create for her with my body when I hold her at night. I've been squeezing a little tighter lately. Hopefully she can feel that I'm still here and she can lean into me as hard and as much as she needs to. We haven't had as much sex lately as we normally do, but I'm ok with that as long as I know she isn't drifting away from me. I think I'm going to take her out. Get her dressed real sexy and drown her in attention. Let her know I'm still here for her. Whatever she needs. She's been dying to see the stage play of The Color Purple. I'm going to grab a couple tickets and make reservations at her favorite restaurant. We've never had an issue connecting and having a blast when we're out, so I expect this time to be no different. I'm going to call Drew and see if he and Mel would like to join us. I know she won't be able to deny a good time with those two tagging along. There's always unstoppable laughter and authentic fun when the four of us are together.

Are you going to tell me where you're taking me now? My wife asked me from the passenger side of my SUV for the third time tonight. I told you it's a surprise.

Now sit back, relax and enjoy the ride. You're going to enjoy it, I promise. Alicia did just as I asked reclining her seat after turning the volume up on the Mint Condition playlist I had softly playing. Moments later we pulled up to the curb in front of the theater. I exited my side of the truck and waived the guy working valet off from opening my wife's door, I got it partner. He threw both hands up to gesture that he didn't mean any disrespect. I gave him a nod that said None taken as I handed him my keys. My wife looked absolutely stunning tonight, especially to say she had no idea what to dress for. I mean, it's amazing that after 15 years with this woman she still possessed the ability to make me say Damn! I held Alicia's hand as she stepped out of the car. Looking up at the marquee reading The Color Purple, a look of shock grabbed ahold of her face and would not let go. I found amusement in her amusement. Allowing her to walk slightly ahead of me as I stole another glance at her from behind I thought to myself, I cannot wait to get her back to our home so that I can peel this dress from her perfectly shaped body and have my way with her; or let her have her way with me. Either way, I don't care. Closing the gap between us I wrapped my arm gently around my wife's waist and softly said to her in her ear,

"I just want you to know that I love and appreciate you. Tonight is about showing you my gratitude."

"Thank you so much baby", Alicia said turning slightly to kiss me on the cheek. "You are most welcome, but don't thank me just yet. The night is still young, anything can happen." Just as I said that I heard my brother in law's voice behind us, "Big Head!"

Alicia

SURPRISE! The room exploded as I entered the private room of the restaurant. Shock covered my face as I grasped at my chest. Because I was lured here under the pretense of a romantic dinner for two, you could imagine my bewilderment when I was welcomed by an alarming surprise from my closest friends and family. I turned around to face my husband who stood behind me wearing a colossal grin on his face. I playfully hit his chest as he pulled me into a tight hug. Normally I hate surprises, but something about this one made my heart smile and burst with joy. Derek's thoughtfulness always amazes me. The thought of all of the time and effort that must have gone into planning and putting this whole thing together made me love him a little more, if that's even possible. Staring into my husband's eyes I couldn't help but gush, "I love you so much. Thank you for this babe."

"You're not upset? I know how much you hate surprises."

"How can I be upset when you've gone through so much trouble to pull this off, and without me finding out about it, no less?"

"It was no trouble at all. That smile on your face makes it all worth it."

"Are you going to hog her all night?", I heard my mom say behind me.

"No ma'am", Derek said letting me go so that I could turn to hug her.

"Hey Ma" I said before kissing her cheek. She squeezed me like she did when we were children. That familiar feeling filling me with nostalgia and causing me to grin with glee. "Happy birthday sweetheart."

"Thank you, Mama."

I felt a smack on my butt. I already knew it was Mel before turning around for confirmation. "Happy birthday, chump!"

"Thank you Mel", I said wrapping my arm around her neck and kissing her cheek.

"I can't believe Derek put all of this together", I stated taking in the room.

"I don't know why. You know that man would do anything to make you happy."

My sister did have a point. It was all just so breathtaking. Music played throughout the room loud enough to enjoy it, but not so loud that people had to yell over it. The room was decorated with lavender and silver balloons and strings of tiny LED lights hung from the ceiling making it appear as though stars lived there. Silver and purple lanterns hung in each corner of the room lending just enough light to complete the ambiance. Crystal vases housing cattleya orchids surrounded by tea candles that sat in crystal dishes served as each table's center piece. I spotted one table covered in decadent desserts. It all looked so beautiful, it was almost a shame that people were going to eat it. I fought back tears as I took it all in. The people I love most all made time to show up for me tonight. Almost as if he sensed my heart filling up, my husband slid his arm around my waist and led me to our table. Come on, let's get some food in you. It was then I noticed servers walking the room with trays of wine, champagne and appetizers. They were all dressed in white button-up shirts tucked inside black pants. Lavender suspenders wrapped their torsos while matching ties hung from their necks. The lady servers had silver flowers tucked in their hair. My husband really thought of everything. Nothing was out of place. Even the servers blended into the decor. I grabbed a glass of wine from a tray as we walked pass a server.

My husband led me to a table where my brother in law sat talking to Derek's best friend, Amir. When Drew saw me walking towards them he jumped up from his seat, and like a big kid grabbed me into a hug that lifted my feet from the ground as he spun around with me in his arms.

"Happy birthday, Big Head", he said enthusiastically while carefully placing my feet back on the floor. One thing I can say about my brother in law is he does not care what is happening, he never misses an opportunity to shower me with love. I couldn't love him more if my mom birthed him.

"Thank you Brother", I said unable to control my laughter. Amir stepped around Drew's massive frame, "Hey Sis. Happy birthday", he said kissing my forehead.

"Thank you", I responded. Derek pulled a seat out for my mother and gently helped slide it under the table after she took her seat. He pulled the chair next to hers out for me.

"Thank you so much baby. I really appreciate you", I stated before kissing his lips.

"This is nothing, just a small token of my love and admiration for you. You deserve this and so much more, but save your thanks for later", he said with a wink of his eye. Forgetting my mom was present I responded, "Oh, don't you worry about that. I fully plan to show you just how grateful I am."

Mom cleared her throat as she took a sip from her champagne glass. Derek chuckled, "Sorry Ma." He walked around to take his seat next to me. Mel, Drew and Amir were all at our table. The rest of the party guests began to take their seats. Once most of the room was seated, the music gradually got lower and lower. With the room quiet for about three seconds beautiful piano music filled the air causing everyone to turn their attention towards the source. Happy birthday to you. Happy birthday to you. I covered my mouth and gasped when I noticed it was Saint Mercedes sitting behind a keyboard singing a slow and deliberate version of Happy Birthday. Catching my reaction she winked in my direction. Looking over at my husband I smiled, "I can't believe this. Saint Mercedes?"

"I know how much you love her."

"This night is too much. What haven't you thought of?"

"There's no such thing. Nothing is too much for you, beautiful."

I sent him a glanced that said You are definitely getting some tonight before turning my attention back to the small stage area where Saint Mercedes played the keys and sang angelically. Her voice stirs my spirit and makes me feel the good kind of anxious inside. She could sing the alphabet and still have my undivided attention. After Happy Birthday, she went into a set of original music fused with covers of some of my favorite songs. Completely submerged in the music I hadn't noticed Derek sliding a velvet box in front of me. I turned to see what was happening when I heard Mel say "OK Brother, I see you." Looking down at the box in front of me before giving my husband a What's this? expression. Without saying a word he smiled a smile that said Just open it. Inside the box was a gorgeous diamond neckless and earring set. Although he surprised me with gifts all the time, I was filled with appreciation and excitement every time. He removed the neckless from the box and draped it around my neck before fastening it.

"Thank you, babe, I love it."

This night really couldn't get any better. I am on surprise overload. I don't know if I could take any more.

Servers began walking the room with trays of food and placing the plates in front of my guests. The food looks amazing. Everyone seem to be enjoying themselves. I doubt anyone is enjoying the night more than me. I'm going to have to bring my A game for Derek's birthday to top this. I'm going to have to pull out all the stops. I'm thinking Eiffel Tower.

Alicia

Don't Answer: Happy birthday my love. I miss you. I need to see you, A.

Sitting at my desk grading papers when I'm suddenly interrupted by the ding of my phone alerting me to a text message. The phrase out of sight out of mind has not rang more true than in this moment right here. I haven't laid eyes on nor have I had any sort of contact with this man since the night I broke things off. Now I'm stuck paralyzed by one text. One single text. 12 words. 14 syllables has caused a tsunami of emotions to come rushing through every nerve ending in my body. I actually thought this was someone I was getting over. I felt like this was a situation I was finally getting pass. But sitting here with my eyes repeatedly reading the text over and over is making me reconsider my entire position. How justify even possible that just five minutes ago I was in a completely different head space? I can hear my grandmother's voice in my head so clear, You never know what's going to happen. She would always say this to Mel and I. Honestly, growing up I didn't get it, but as an adult I understand all too well. Life can throw you a plot twist at the drop of a dime. You never know what is going to happen. One minute I'm feeling pretty good, happy even, which I haven't been in a while. Now I'm questioning all of the thoughts and feelings I've experienced over this past month. How do I respond to this? Do I even bother? I don't want to have to deal with this at all. My heart and head are in a tug of war. My head is saying to delete the text and get back to work. My heart, on the other hand, is screaming Tell him you love him. Tell him you miss his too. Tell him you need to see him as well. Why are you fighting what you instinctively feel? Just lean into it. If you love him, say so.

My heart wins the battle.

Me: I love you. I miss you.

An involuntary sigh leaves my body after hitting the SEND button.

Don't Answer: I need to see you

****

After knocking on the door, a feeling of apprehension swept through me. What was I doing here? I've been on autopilot since I read his last message. Without giving it a second thought I tossed the papers I was grading into my briefcase, grabbed my keys and headed to the faculty parking lot for my Audi. I don't even remember the drive over here, but standing here waiting for my honey to come to the door I'm fully aware. Consciousness is present. Before I could give in to hesitation the door swung open and I stood face to face with the man I've tried so hard to forget existed. He stood before me a pair of basketball shorts and tattoos. His expression saying he was expecting me. I inhaled his scent and before I could make heads or tails of any of this my lips were on his. His arms were around my waist and mine around his neck. I'm not sure who kissed who first, but like magnets we were cemented. I couldn't pull away from him. Honestly, in this moment, I didn't want to. I'm swimming in him and nothing else in the world matters. In this moment my heart released tension I wasn't even aware it was holding.

Alicia

f I could stay away from this man, I would. I know it's wrong, but it's like he's some sort of addiction that I can't break free of. His eyes, his smile, his mind, his body, his smell, his touch, the sound of his voice; I can't get enough of him. He lures me in in ways I never thought possible. Our chemistry is deeper than you could imagine. I think what makes it so difficult, is it's not just sex between us. If it were just sex, I could walk away. Sex would be easy. But what began as a fervent kiss on a crowded dance floor has evolved into a connection I can't see myself living without.

I see my honey walking across the parking lot to meet me at our favorite restaurant for lunch. Even his walk is appealing. I love this place for the sidewalk dining area and the margaritas.

"Hi honey", I say greeting him with a kiss.

"Hello gorgeous. I can't believe you made it here before me. It must be expected to storm today."

"Ha ha ha, very funny. Today is predicted to be a lovely day, I'll have you know."

He grinned deeply showing off those beautiful white teeth and the dimple in his right cheek.

"I'm just playing. How was your morning? Have a good run?"

"I did, actually. My morning was pretty good. Thank you for asking. How was yours?"

"Not too bad. I had a really good workout, washed my truck and had a relaxing shower. I'm just happy I get to spend some time with you today."

"Ditto."

The waitress walked over to our table carrying a bowl of what smelled like fresh baked bread. She placed the bowl on the table in between my honey.

"Hi, my name is Sam and I'll be your server today. Can I start you guys off with some drinks?"

"I'll have a basil lemon drop, and she'll have a top shelf peach margarita."

I couldn't help but to smile grandiosely across the table at him. I loved it when he did that.

"Thank you baby."

He grinned and winked in my direction.

After lunch, my honey and I decided to take stroll on the beach. We don't usually get a lot of time like this. It's usually a couple of hours here, an hour or two there. Being here with him like this almost makes me forget that I am a married woman. Things are just so easy with him.

Not that things are difficult with Derek, or even that I'm unhappy in my marriage, because that couldn't be further from the truth. I'm just a woman who finds herself in love with two men. I love my husband unconditionally, until death do us part. I just so happen to also uncontrollably love this beautiful man holding my hand on this beach.

It's something tranquil about the cool breeze by the water blowing through my hair, feeling the sand between my toes, and watching my honey be completely vulnerable with me. He never shies away from expressing how he feels or sharing what's on his mind. I love that he feels secure enough with me to open up and allow me to share in his world, even if it's only for a few moments at a time.

In the distance I noticed a tall, brown skinned, bearded guy taking pictures. Warily I paused with caution.

"What's wrong? You ok?", my honey asks noticing the decline in my stride.

"Do you see that guy up ahead taking pictures? What if he snaps a pic of us?"

"So what if he does? He's a complete stranger. In fact, I think he should want to capture a sight as gorgeous as you."

"Cut the Rico Suave act", I said with annoyance in my voice. "That's easy for you to say. I'm the one with everything to lose."

He stopped short and spun around to face me. Grasping my apprehension he gave me and incredulous look before speaking. "Babe, calm down. I didn't mean it like that. You know I take our inconspicuousness seriously. It's just a guy taking photos on a beach. Are you really that nervous?"

"He could be a private investigator. You never know."

"Listen, babe, I work with private investigators all the time. All out in the public eye isn't really their thing. In fact, it kind of goes against the nature of the job. Their work is ineffective if people knew they were being watched."

My face and shoulders relaxed a bit taking in his rationality. The sudden feeling of paranoia fleeing, "I'm sorry honey. I may have overreacted."

He held up his hand illustrating little space between his thumb and pointer finger, "Just a little."

I smirked and playfully hit his chest, "Not funny, jerk."

He chuckled as he swooped me up into his arms twirling me around once before putting me down. "Let's go face the big bad monster so you can see there's nothing to be afraid of", he said taking my hand leading me in the direction of the tall bearded.

"Hey man, what's up?", My honey said fearlessly walking up to the guy as if he knew him.

"Hello", the guy said warily looking at my honey.

"I know this might be a bit weird, but do you mind settling something for us. My girl noticed you taking pictures. Now her money is on you being a P.I. I'm betting on you being a photographer."

Mouth opened in disbelief, I starred at the side of my honey's face. Any other time his spontaneity is adorable, but I'm failing to find anything adorable about it now that it's motivated at my expense. The bearded guy chuckled a bit before stating, "Photographer."

My honey gave me a smirk that hid behind a face that said he was trying not to say I told you so. I hit his arm, "You really are a jerk."

Letting go of the laugh he'd been holding back, "And you still love me, so I'm ok with that."

I playfully sneered at him

"You guys are cute", the bearded guy chimed in.

My honey asked, "Would you mind taking our picture?"

"Not at all. It's what I do."

"Any particular pose you recommend?"

"I don't want you to pose at all. Just act natural like I'm not even here."

And so we did. We walked a small stretch along the shore holding hands as we were before we noticed the photographer. My honey cracked jokes that made me laugh organically. He wrapped his arms around my waist and picked me up. No spinning this time, he just kissed me. Kissed me so passionately I almost forgot we were not alone. He put me down and took note of the aroused expression I now wore on my face. We walked back over to the photographer. My honey asked, "How much do you charge for the prints?"

"I'll tell you what, I'm in the process of rebuilding my website and am out shooting fresh material. Let me use the pics we took today for my website and in exchange I'll send you the prints."

Now it was my honey's turn to shoot me a skeptic glance. With my spontaneity waking up to play with his I replied, "Sure. You have a deal Mr..."

"Corey. Corey Anthony."

I extended my hand to shake Corey's, "Alicia. It was nice to meet you Corey."

"Nice to meet you as well."

My honey asked, "Do you have a card?"

Corey reached into his pocket and pulled out a steel card holder with the initials CA engraved on the front and handed us one of the cards from inside of it.

"Awesome, I'll get with you so that we can set up where to send the prints and all that good stuff."

"Sounds like a plan. Thank y'all."

"Thank you. Enjoy the rest of your day." I said before grabbing my honey's hand.

"Likewise", Corey stated before turning to raise his lens as if our whole interaction never took place.

Alicia

"We're going see Mariah! We're going see Mariah!", Mel is yelling into my ear on the other side of the phone line.

"What are you talking about, Mel? Calm down and use full sentences."

"I won two free tickets for me and a guest to go see Mariah Carey on her Caution tour at the Beau Rivage in Biloxi, Mississippi!"

"What! When?"

"Tomorrow night."

"Oh my gosh! We're going see Mariah! We're going see Mariah!", I sang on my side of the line. "I have to go figure out what I'm wearing, what I'm going to do with my hair. I can't believe this." Now I'm the one who needs to calm down. Mel knows how much I love Mariah. We've been super fans since Fantasy. We love the earlier stuff like Vision of Love and Hero and Emotions, but she got us on the hook, never to be taken off with that Fantasy track.

"I'm leaving the kids with Drew and we can hit the road right after work."

"That sounds like a plan."

"Who's driving?"

"You now that doesn't matter to me."

"Ok, I'll pick you up at your house for 6:30 and we'll head out."

"Sounds good."

"See you tomorrow Sis."

"Laters", we end the call.

This has set the tone for the rest of my day. I am over the moon with excitement. Not that I was in a bad mood before, but now I'm ecstatic. So excited, I can't wait until I get home to share the news with my husband, I have to call him now.

****

I hear the music blaring from my sister's car as she pulls into my driveway. She's late, as usual. Derek and I instinctively look at one another and say Mel's here. I grab my bag and my husband walks me out to the car. He opens the door and walks out to greet Mel, It's amazing you're still able to hear anything the way you listen to your music.

"Music is only made to be listened to one way. Loudly", Mel laughs.

Derek shook his head and let out a soft laugh as he walked around to the passenger side of the car to open my door. I squeezed his neck tight and kissed him as if I would never see him again.

"Ok you two. That's enough, we're going to miss the show at this rate."

"If we miss the show, it won't be because I kissed my husband goodbye", I said sliding into the car.

"You ladies have fun", Derek said as he closed the car door.

"Oh, we will!", Mel yelled backing out of the driveway.

I watched as my husband faded into our home when a text message came through on my phone.

My honey: Hey woman. How's your day going?

"Oh no. There will be no male distractions tonight. Let your honey know you are not available for him tonight. It's my time", Mel said never taking her eyes off the road ahead.

"And how do you know that was my honey?"

"Telepathy."

"Whatevs."

"Who was it then?"

I dropped my head and mumbled, "My honey."

"What was that? I didn't quite hear you all the way."

"Fine, it was my honey."

"Mmm hm, I know. Now tell him you're off the grid tonight."

I swear, Mel can be so bossy at times. It's like she forgets I'm the big sister. I do as she says, not because she said so, but because I have been looking forward to this time with my sister since she called screaming into my ear yesterday.

As Mel races down the interstate, we talk about things that make us laugh, things we forgot used to make us laugh, and things at least one of us wishes the other would forget. After only an hour and 45 minutes, we reach our destination. This is the first time either of us have been to the Beau Rivage, so we take in all of the sights on our walk to find the theater. We make it to will call and collect our tickets. The lady working will call informs us that we made it just in time because the show was getting ready to start and she was just about to close up for the night. She offered to walk us to our seats and we graciously accepted her kindness. From the will call counter we could hear Mariah belting out Always Be My Baby, another favorite of ours. We excitedly followed our escort into the theater and down the first section of stairs. Not sure where our seats were located, we anxiously followed the benevolent lady until we reached the seventh row on the floor. We thanked the casino worker and began to slide down the aisle past the concert goers who managed to make it here on time until we reached our seats. We settled in and took in the atmosphere of the theater while trying to grasp ahold of the reality that Mariah Carey was just feet away from us singing one of our favorite songs.

Song after song, our excitement overflowed. We commented on all of the beautiful dresses Mariah changed into, sang and danced in our seats, yelled out things like That's my song and Come on Mariah. The audience was told to remain seated throughout the show. I guess so that everyone would be able to see and enjoy the show fully, but by the end of the show Mariah was performing Vision of Love. This must have been a crowd favorite, because before long Mel and most of the audience were on their feet and swaying along. I could have lived in these moments forever, but like the rest of us, Mariah has other obligations so we must say goodnight.

After the final song and the crowd disbursed a little, Mel and I began to make our way out of the theater. We followed the crowd of lambs out of the theater and into the casino where everyone broke out into different directions. Mel and I made several notes on our way in of places we wanted to stop at on our way back, Haagen-Dazs being one. That stop was really for me. If I created a list of my favorite things like Oprah, Haagen-Dazs Butter Pecan ice cream would be at the top of it. Mel wanted to stop and grab something to eat. Once I got my triple scoop of butter pecan in a sweet waffle cone, I didn't care what we did. We made it to the Haagen-Dazs shop just before they were to close for the night. I already knew what I wanted, but Mel was surrounded by a copious amount of chilled sweet delectables and it was hard for her decide on a flavor. After receiving my cone I headed over to the register to pay. I told the cashier to ring up whatever my sister decided to get as well. After what felt like an hour, Mel finally had her frozen concoction in her hand made up of who the hell knows what. She had a little bit of everything in her bowl. Mel walked over to the register, not knowing I had paid already. When the cashier informed her that her ice cream had been taken care of already, Mel walked my way with a face that said Why did you do that?

"I was going to pay." I shrugged my shoulders at her and turned to leave the shop. I heard her say out loud to herself that she was paying for the food. I chuckled to myself.

      We found a delectable little café just around the way from the ice cream shop. Apparently, the rest of the lambs had the same idea because they had no tables available. Not in any hurry to do much of anything, Mel and I took the buzzer that would alert us once a table became available. While we waited, we ate our ice cream and chatted. We took pictures of each other and with each other, courtesy of a guy standing nearby who offered to take our picture so that we would have some together. We chatted some more about everything and nothing. Finally, our buzzer went off letting us know we could head back to the café for our table. Once seated, we grabbed the menus to see what grabbed our attention. I went for the turkey burger with French fries and settled on a sweet margarita drink fairly quickly, while Mel couldn't decide what she wanted. Ultimately, just as she had done in the Haagen-Dazs she had Jason, our waiter, bring her a little bit of everything.

      We sat in the fancy decorated café doing more talking and sipping than eating. We relished in the night and how perfect it had all been. We couldn't have had a better time even if we had planned it. I love it when things just divinely fall into place as they should. We ended up with to-go boxes for everything we ordered. When Jason brought the check over I grabbed it from his hand and quickly slid my card into the flap. When I went on hand it back to him, Mel reached for it before he could grab ahold of it and reminded me that she was paying. I didn't forget her little comment from earlier, I just chose to ignore it. I wanted to treat her, but my sister was dead set on treating me. I took the check from her to hand it back to Jason when she ordered him not to take my card. There goes that bossiness again. Jason, who probably doesn't get to witness this sort of disagreement often, just stood there confused. Not sure whether to take the check with the card that was already inside or to wait to see which way this argument landed. He opted for the latter. Eventually, I decided to concede and let Mel pay. I could tell Mel was prepared for us to remain at this impasse the rest of the night if she had to, so for Jason's sake, I let her pay.

We grabbed our bag of leftovers and headed out of the café. On our way to the elevators that led to the parking garage Mel caught a glimpse of a huge water fountain with a bunch of extravagant lights flashing around it and decided we had to take more pictures by the fountain. Just as we did inside, we snapped pictures of ourselves and a couple who stood by with the same idea as Mel offered to take our picture together. In exchange to thank them for their kind gesture, Mel offered to take a couple photos of them. At this point, I'm freezing by this water and can't wait to get back inside the building where it's warm and inside the car.

When we made it down to the parking garage Mel offered to drive back. I don't fight her on this.

Alicia

Today is such a beautiful day. The sky is clear, sun is out, It's not too hot and there's a soft gentle breeze every so often. I live for days like this. Especially when I don't have to be cooped up indoors. I got to spend the morning shopping with my sister, which I'm always grateful for any moment I get to share with her. Now I'm in my Audi, with my shades on, flying down the street that wraps around the park. I've been running on the trail near my house lately, so I haven't had the pleasure of running through the park and taking in its beauty. I was tempted to go for a few laps just because the day is gorgeous, but I'm enjoying cruising with nowhere in particular to run off to. Derek's been working hard to win the case he's working on. He has court all day, so I decide not to bother him and enjoy my me time.

Mary J is blasting through my car speakers adding the soundtrack to what is turning out to be a perfect day. This is one of my happy songs. The moment it comes on with its addictive beat and melody, I can't help but to turn it up and dance. Behind my tinted windows I'm now in my own world dancing and singing right along with her

That's why I don't mind saying I love you…

I'm loving this feeling of just enjoying life right now when Mary & I are interrupted by someone calling. I yell, "Damn Bluetooth!" Looking down at the screen I see it's my honey calling. Quickly my mood shifts from sudden annoyance to sheer excitement. Anxious to hear his voice, I told the car to answer the call.

"Hello"

"Hello Beautiful, how's your day going?"

"Well, just when I thought it couldn't get any better one of my favorite people called. How's your day treating you?"

"Better now that I'm hearing your voice. I can't wait to see you."

"We'll just have to see what we can do about that then, now won't we?"

"What are you getting into?"

"Just wandering around in my car, enjoying this admirable day. What do you have in mind?"

"Something simple & relaxing. Dinner maybe. A movie. Both perhaps."

"Sounds great! I'll head home to shower and get changed. Meet you at your house in about an hour?"

"You got it. See you soon, A."

"Ok my love..."

Caught off guard by what looks like a silver car flying in my direction, I cut my sentence short. The driver doesn't seem to know where their brakes are. Before I had a chance to swerve out of the way, my world started spinning. Literally, everything around me was spinning before my eyes. Trees, people, cars, buildings, the sky. I saw it all in one big whirlwind. My mind trying desperately to put together what was happening to no prevail. Suddenly, the world stopped. My world was dark. Black. I saw nothing. I heard nothing. Unsure of how long the darkness lasted, I languidly began to hear what sounded like faint sirens. My eyes began to open and I can see what I think is flashing lights, but I'm not sure. My mind is back to trying to figure out what is going on. I think I was in a car accident. That can't be it. I don't feel any pain, albeit I can't move either. And nothing is in the correct position. I see people running in my direction, but they're all upside down. Now I begin to freak out from fear. Am I going to die? What is happening? Can someone call my husband? My hon...

Alicia

Drifting in and out of consciousness, through barely slitted lights flashed rapidly over my head. I can hear lots of people yelling, but I can't make out what anyone is saying. I feel pain in my left leg. It's all I can feel. I can't move my body. I'm trying to ask someone what is happening. It's almost like they don't hear me at all. Now that I think about it, I can't hear me either. I can't speak. Frightened, I begin to cry. I can't make sense of anything that's taking place right now. My mind is struggling to put the pieces together. The last thing I remember is hearing Mary... I was hit! Crashed! In the park! Someone needs to call my husband.

There are people swarming all around me. They all appear to be going about their own business, yet working together. I catch a glimpse of a white coat with Javon Johnson, MD stitched on the upper left side. I take it she's the doctor in charge. The darkskinned lady in glasses with a big afro, chubby cheeks and a gap in between her front teeth flashed a bright light in my face and asked me to follow it with my eyes. I followed the light left, and then right. "Good! My name is Doctor Johnson. Can you tell me your name?"

In my head I tell her my name is Alicia.

"Can you tell me what happened to you?"

I don't understand why the words aren't coming out of my mouth.

"Do you know where you are?"

I heard myself say "The hospital."

"Ok. Her speech is slurred. Let's get her up for a head CT."

A head CT? What is happening? This is not how I envisioned my afternoon going. My husband must be worried sick about me. I haven't touched base with him since this morning. We never go this long without checking-in. I'm not sure of the time, but it feels like an entire day has passed. I have to get to my phone. I have to let him know I'm all right. Am I all right?

"We're going to take really good care of you. You've been in an accident. From what I can tell so far, your leg is broken, but there doesn't seem to be any internal injuries. I'm ordering a head CT to make sure there's no brain trauma we need to be concerned about, and I'm going to get you something for the pain. Is there anyone you need us to call?"

"My husband."

"You got it, Alicia. Just relax. I know this is all kind of scary, but I promise I'm going to take really good care of you."

Derek

The only part about the drive to the hospital I remember is me praying. I know I drove myself here, but I don't remember the drive itself. What streets I took to get here or what landmarks I passed on the way here. My mind kept replaying the voice on the phone, "Mr. Simpson, this is Ashley... Hospital... We have your wife here... Accident." I felt it in my gut all day that something terrible was going to happen today. The second those words left Ashley's mouth, fear rose through my body. Hot, tingly, suffocating fear. My worst fear. Losing my wife. I've loved that woman since we were freshmen in college. Feels like a lifetime. She's my life. My everything. Our lives have been so intertwined for the last seven years I don't even know how I would function without her. How I would breath without her.

Bursting through those double doors, I spelled that familiar scent of alcohol and disinfectant that reminded you immediately you were in a hospital. A place capable of provoking a copious range of emotions. I always found it fascinating that a single place can render so many different feelings and memories. On one hand it can be the place a couple brings their first born into the world. A joyous occasion filled with love, smiles and gratitude. A beautiful new born baby being born to parents whose only wish now is to love and protect them. Then on the other hand, a hospital can also be the place you watch someone you hold dearest to your heart close their eyes and take their final breath. A place that closes the chapter on a life you've spent all your life loving.

In this case that scent would forever be linked to the day I got the call that my wife had been in an accident. Maybe I was being paranoid. Maybe I was blowing the whole thing out of proportion. Maybe my wife is fine. Maybe I'll walk into her room and she'll be sitting up watching bad television. But I couldn't shake the fact that the hospital's nurse called me. Not my wife. It wasn't my wife calling to say babe, I've been in an accident, but I'm ok. It was the nurse. Why didn't my wife call me if she was ok? If she were just in here because it's routine after a fender bender, why hadn't she picked up the phone to say so herself?

Derek

"Hi, my name is Derek Simpson. I got a call saying my wife is here."

Before the guy sitting behind the nurses' station could answer, a girl with long blonde hair pulled back into a ponytail appeared from what seemed like nowhere saying, "Mr. Simpson! I'm Ashley, I spoke to you over the phone. I can bring you back to your wife."
I walked behind Ashley following her lead down the hospital halls. My focus on her bouncing ponytail as it swung from side to side. I was afraid to bring my attention to anything else because it was all I could do to hold my shit together. Fearing the worst, I followed Ashley into a section of the hospital that resembled an intensive care unit. Ashley slowed her stride and turned around to face me, "Your wife is right through those doors, Mr. Simpson."
Afraid to ask, my voice trembled as the words trickled out of my mouth, "How is she?"

"She sustained a concussion, a few broken ribs and a fractured leg. We're monitoring her for a potential brain bleed, but all things considered your wife is a very lucky woman. I was told that her vehicle flipped over a

ENTANGLED

few times after being struck head on by another driver.
I've seen my share of car accidents and believe me, Mr.
Simpson, this had all the makings to be so much worse.
We have her sedated, but you can go back and sit with
her."

"Thank you."

I began walking towards my wife's room. Through
the giant window looking into the room, I saw my wife was
not alone. Focused on the unexpected visitor, I realized
it was Amir. I called Mel and mama on the drive over to
let them know about the accident and what hospital
Alicia had been taken to, but I hadn't reached out to my
brother yet. So what is he doing here? How is he here
before me? Why is it he's here unbeknownst to me? Why
hadn't he called me to say he was coming? Hell, if he
knew my wife had been in an accident and was laying in
someone's hospital, why hadn't he called to tell me that.
The closer I got to the room, the more confusion and
anger began to replace my fear and heartbreak. A
thousand questions swirled through my mind as if they
were a merry go round going one hundred miles an hour.

Once I was right outside the window of Alicia's
room I was able to see my best friend hunched over my
wife's bed. Is he crying? He appears broken. Trying to
make sense of what I'm seeing, my eyes dart around the

room. When my eyes focused on my best friend holding my wife's hand as he cried over her bedside, bells went off in my head like the Disney World fireworks show. Hindsight reels began flashing through my memory. The night I got home from one of my business trips and noticed the bed appeared to not have been slept in. The day my wife hadn't checked in for hours and I couldn't get her on the phone, I couldn't get ahold of Amir either. The seemingly unwarranted despondent mood of my wife a couple months ago. In my reflection I can see that Amir wasn't doing so hot around that time either. My attention had been so fixed on my wife's well-being that the subtle change in my brother's emotional state hadn't even registered with me. The strange glances and body language of the both of them at Alicia's birthday party. Although, it hadn't appeared strange then, looking back on it now makes me question how long has my brother been fucking my wife and exactly how deep did this go. This has been my best friend since we shared a college dorm room our freshman year. We've been in the trenches together. Experienced the happiest moments of our lives together. This guy knows where all the bodies are buried. This is my brother. Thicker than blood. I could never bring myself to betray him like this. To invade a space so personal. So sacred. A relationship regarded with so much appreciation. He knows, almost better than my wife, how I feel about her. For it all to come to this. I couldn't have seen this coming in a million years. My heart instantly broke into a million pieces that sank to the pit of my stomach. Anger rose from my hurt. I needed answers.

Alicia

Floating just under an anesthetic haze, I thought I heard my husband's voice. My eyes fluttered a bit ask felt myself being relinquished from the drowsy hold of whatever meds this hospital had me on. I could hear what sounded like complete chaos. Derek must be watching TV. I wish he'd turn it down. We are not at home, and whatever he's watching is way too loud for a hospital room. I struggle to speak so that I could tell Derek he needs to turn the volume down so that he doesn't disturb anyone else.

"Fuck you boy!", even with so much malice hugging his tone I would recognize that sexy voice any where. That voice that sent a tingle through my limbs each and every time I heard it. But I can't say I've ever heard it utter such words with so much venom. What was he doing here? Who was he yelling at?

"Fuck you!"

I gasped hard enough to inhale the entire room. I know that to be the voice of the man I've loved since college. Hearing both the voice of my honey and my husband yelling angrily at each other told me one thing. My secret was out. My life as I've known it is over. Finally able to shake the anesthesia enough to open my eyes. I was accosted by my husband in the face of his best friend screaming vileness wrapped in animosity and anguish. His face contorted and saliva spraying from his mouth accompanying every other word, I don't even recognize him. Who is this man? When he turned his attention towards me, I wasn't sure if I should attempt to run, find something to defend myself with, or beg and plead with him until he understood how sorry I was. His gaze transforming from pure hatred to a look of deep sadness. I could see in parts of his face that he was extremely angry, but his eyes wanted to cry. This broke my heart. Just knowing that I did this to him. My selfishness did this to him. Caused this entire shit show to play out like this. I opened my mouth to speak when Derek beat me to it.

"All I've ever did was love you, Alicia. I've loved you with every cell in my body for as long as I've known you. My best friend?", he asked as if he was still trying to make sense of all of this. Amir walked over to the side of my bed, "A, we don't have to hide any more. Tell him you love me. Tell him you want to be with me. Tell him!" I shut my eyes, but even in my momentary blindness I recognized the sound of a blow. My eyes flying open in shock, I saw Amir moving his hand away from the side of his face and throw a blow of his own towards Derek. In the very next second all hell broke loose. I could not believe what I was seeing. The men I loved engaged in what looked like a street fight to the death. Horrified, I tried to yell for them to stop. Tried to call for help, but they were so enveloped in this now bloody brawl that I may as well had been whispering. My voice carrying no weight whatsoever. Where were the nurses? Security? Somebody? Why weren't there anyone around to break this up? Surely, someone heard the commotion. I couldn't believe what I was seeing. The pain in my leg let me know this was not a dream. I reached for the remote to page a nurse when I heard the loudest crash. Amir had grabbed ahold of Derek and slammed him into the giant window overlooking the nurses station. Glass shattering all over the place. Speechless, I sat still in my hospital bed. I was sure someone had to hear that and was on the way. My honey looked down at his best friend as he lied there on the floor covered in glass. Glancing over in my direction he opened his mouth to speak when suddenly from out in the hallway I heard, "I need some help over here!"

The both of our attention spinning toward where Derek lied lifeless. I watched as a river of blood streamed and pooled around my husband's head. I sat up and tried to run to him, forgetting I wasn't able to use my legs just yet because of the fracture in my left leg.

"DEREK!", I screamed.

I watched the man I've shared my life with for 15 years lying completely still on the floor. Doctors and nurses flooded the area where he lied in a matter of seconds.

"Derek, baby, get up! Please get up!", I cried and pleaded with my husband. Begged God to let him be ok. The crew of doctors and nurses lifted Derek up onto a gurney. Albeit, no one said anything, as they were all attempting to save my husband's life, I knew. I knew he had taken his final breath. I didn't need for anyone to confirm it. His face a blank stare. Free of any emotion. No anger, sadness, pain, nothing. Just a face absent of any trace of life that would signify he was still amongst the land of the living. I knew God hadn't answered my prayer. I screamed out in uncontrollable horror. This has to be a dream. Someone is going to walk into my room and wake me from this dream any minute now. Only no one came. I watched helplessly as the man whose single touch sent tingles through my body on more occasions than I can count took the life out of the man that I've loved since before we really knew what love was.

The crew of doctors and nurses rolled the gurney out of the room. I'm left laying here with no way to atone for the things I've done, I'll never have the chance to make it up to him. He'll never know how sorry I am for causing him so much pain. Out in the hallway, I watched as my honey was escorted away by two men in dark blue police uniforms. Hands cuffed behind his back and his face filled with shame and anguish. My heart broke for him too. I know I did that to him. I know I did all of this. I had the power to stop all of this before we reached this point in our lives, but I allowed myself to get carried away. I allowed myself to get caught up in pleasure. Never, truly, realizing what my actions were setting into motion. Now I lay here in this hospital bed with the final moments of my life blowing up before my eyes playing in my mind on repeat. Suddenly, I could hear that conversation with Mama as if she were standing in front of me now. I should have listened. Why couldn't I have just stayed away?

Alicia

Alicia, what in God's name is going on? That was Mama entering the room yelling incredulously. Mama and Mel arrived at the hospital shortly after all of the chaos erupted. I stared into the faces of my mother and sister searching my mind for the words to explain what just happened. I searched for the words to tell my mother and sister that Derek was dead. This reality hadn't exactly settled upon me yet, so I had no idea how I was going to explain to them that it was my actions that had sent this calamity crashing down on our family. My mind and body lay in this hospital bed completely numb. Wrapped in grief, shame and guilt as if they were sewn together to make a blanket, I cried. My body shook and I cried. I cried for my loss. I cried for my family's loss. I cried for my actions that led to this moment. I cried until I had nothing left to cry. Despite the turmoil I had caused, I felt four arms swarm me. Four familiar arms I would know blindfolded. The arms of my mama and my sister wrapped around my deflated body and we all cried. Their tears magnified my guilt because I know if not for my greed, lust and incessant need to be enveloped in all things Amir there would be no need for their tears. My mother's son would here. Mel and Drew's brother would be here. My nieces would still have their uncle Derek. I would still have my love. His large frame would be squished in this bed next to me telling me how much he loves me and reassuring me that my body will heal in time. But my selfishness has made this impossible. Now I wonder how much time will be needed to mend my broken heart. This reality crushes me. Leaves me feeling lifeless. I feel like Mortal Kombat's Scorpion has snatched my heart from my chest and finished me.

Alicia

I don't remember Mel coming to get me from the hospital. I don't remember being discharged. I don't remember the ride home. Life has been a blur of flashing lights since that night in the hospital. One day after the next, they all seem to be the same. It's gotten so that I can't tell them apart. From the moment that window shattered and I watched as the life left my husband's body, life appears as though everyone and everything in it is moving at the speed of light while I'm moving in ultra slow motion. I no longer see faces or hear voices. I simply see blurs of shapes and shadows. I hear white noise where voices and music used to be. It's like being on a crowded train moving 1 million miles per hour, unable to decipher one sound from another or make out any one thing. I suppose I set these wheels in motion with my avariciousness. Lord knows if I could take it all back, I would. If I had it to do over again, I would choose my husband as he chose me. I use to believe that life had a way of getting better after the storms passed, but my world is so cloudy these days, I can't see my way out of this personal hell I'm in. I have no idea how life will get better, if life will get better. I'm left to wallow in all of my should've would've could'ves, which is absolutely moot at this point.

I've been going through the motions, trying to regain some sense normalcy. I'm still on leave from work, but I've been slowly trying to put what pieces left of my life back together. I went for a short run this morning. I felt a minuscule piece of comfort in that, but mostly it saddened me. I thought about that old couple in the park and how Derek and I will never get to experience that. I thought about my husband and how I'll never have the opportunity to see him again. Touch him, smell him, wallow in his presence ever again. I thought about the two lives I've ruined. I thought about my actions and how the right amount of bad decisions can send you down a rabbit hole you never want to see the inside of. Emotionally, I was unable to take anymore. I ended my run after only two miles.

I went home and showered before heading to my doctor's appointment. I wasn't up for a doctor's visit today, but I've been rescheduling and putting it off for weeks. I decided I would make it to this one if it's the only thing I accomplish today. A lot of what Dr. Clayton said sounded like the all too familiar white noise for most of the visit; in fact, most of the visit is a mere haze to me. I remember signing in, peeing in a cup, and hearing the words You're pregnant. Somehow, I made it home in one piece, because I sure as hell don't remember how I got here. I've been sitting in this chair for what feels like days. I've completely lost track of time. I'm not even sure what time of day it is. I have no idea how my life came to this. One minute I'm excited about life and happier beyond my wildest dreams. I had the love of my life, and the man of my dreams, or at least the man I thought at the time to be the man of my dreams. Life couldn't get any better. Now, the love of my life lies still in a box. I can never see his face or hear his voice again. The man of my dreams sits in a box incapable of seeing the light of day. Not truly. These days, I can't see his face or hear his voice, because he reminds me of how atrociously things have turned out, and how life will never be the same. However, I do feel the need to reach out to him and get some things off my chest.

Alicia

Three months later...

Amir,

I don't even know where to begin. How is it possible that, literally, one minute life is perfect. You're enjoying a beautiful day, high on love; and in the very next moment all hell has broken out and your life as you've known it is shattered and completely unrecognizable? I don't even recognize the people we are now. Like we're all strangers. I wouldn't have imagined that this is how our story would have played out in a million years. Every day I try to remember what my life was. Try to grasp at what was once familiar to me. And every day I fail. I often think, was it all worth it? I won't diminish what we had to just sex and ask if a few orgasms were worth the price we've payed, but at the same time I want to know. Was my greed and selfishness worth it? Was my desire to have my cake and eat it too worth the chaos that came from it all? My husband is dead and you are in prison. So no. I guess the answer is No. Nothing is worth that. You've lost your freedom and my husband lost his life. The guilt I feel knowing my actions set all of this into motion consumes me. It keeps me up at night. It causes anxiety and panic attacks during the day. How do I pick up what pieces are left of my life and move forward? How do I create a new normal when I don't even know myself any more? I don't trust myself any more. Every move I make, my decision-making abilities come into question. Where I once was a carefree spirit moving where the mood took me, is now replaced with grief, paranoia, and guilt. If only I possessed the ability to go back in time and change things. Knowing what I know now, I'm sure I would do things completely different. I know we aren't what we were and will never be again. I just wanted you to know that I don't blame you. It's taken me a long while to arrive to this place. I blamed you for so long. I was furious with you for taking my husband away from me. Finally, one day I found the courage to do what I had been dreading and avoiding. I faced myself in the mirror. I acknowledged my wrong-doings, and how my actions set us all on this course. Although it takes two, I had the power to stop it. I had the power to say No from the very beginning and stop it before it ever began. In fact, I had a responsibility to stop it. I had a responsibility to end it before it ever began. I failed at that. I failed miserably. So with no magic abilities to rewind time, I'm left with the fallout of the decisions I made. I'm left with hard life lessons. I'm taking life as I know it day by day until the resemblance of normalcy returns to it. My hope is that one day I will feel comfortable in my own skin again, and will be able to trust myself again. My hope is that we both find peace. That you and I find a way to forgive ourselves and find peace. This'll probably be the last time you hear from me, as I need time and space for my own healing. I wish you all the best.

Forever in my prayers

A

Alicia

Alicia,

My mind often drifts back to when we first began. You and Derek had broken up after college and I ran into you at Club Deshay. I knew better than to invade your space, but seeing you so turnt up on the dance floor, completely carefree, impulsively pulled me in your direction. My intuition screaming for me to turn around, grab another chick, hell go home. Anything opposite of walking up to you to join in on your private party. But at the same time, I felt compelled to be near you. Couldn't turn away. That fierce gravitational pull has been my driving force since that day in the club. My body in perfect motion with yours. Evading feelings of awkwardness and unfamiliarity, it felt natural for you to be in my arms. For your hands to be touching my body. For my lips to end up on yours. Uncertain whether it was the alcohol or chemistry, however weirdness nor forbiddance dwelled between us that night. Sure my mind kept reminding me that I was going against every aspect that brokered trust between my brother and I, but it was as if my body needed you. Craved you. And I knew I should have backed off when you guys got back together, especially after he proposed to you, but as much as I wanted to and very well knew I should I couldn't. You already had my heart and I felt as if I would die without you. I knew what we were doing wasn't fair to Derek and I should have wanted more for myself than to be submerged in love with my best friend's wife, but that damn pull just wouldn't release me. Wouldn't let me go seek a woman of my own. People often think it's just women that get themselves caught up in ridiculous situations that they know to be dead ends that won't end well, but I'm man enough to admit men get caught up too.

When I think about the way things played out. What this relationship costed me. Costed us. When I'm reminded how I'll never stick my head in my brother's office door again. How we'll never meet up at the basketball court. How I'll never be able to pick the phone up and call him when I need him. Grief cripples me all over again. But when I look around and am hit with the realization that I'm in here because I took the life of my brother, my best friend in the whole wide world, my mind, body and spirit are all consumed with heartbreak, depression and sorrow. The words don't even exist that would allow me to ever express my apologies. I can't even begin to fathom a string of words that would justify the catastrophe I've brought to your world.

It's astonishing to me how in what feels like the blink of an eye we were drenched in sweat making out on the dance floor of Club Deshay and in the very next instance Derek is dead and I'm writing you a letter from prison. The zeitgeist of the beginning in comparison to where we are now is completely different worlds. It feels like the two don't exist in the same universe. I can see the dominoes falling in my mind. I can almost reach out and touch the moments that led us here, they're so vivid in my thoughts. I question whether I would do anything different if presented with the opportunity. It's a question I don't have the answer to. Not a definitive answer anyway. I know this sounds crazy given our current situation, but when I think back on the time I got to spend with you my heart swells to the point I think it's going to burst. Having had the honor of being loved by you, touched by you, kissed by you, held by you, to have known you at all fills me with gratitude. I apologize if this letter is coming across as sinister or insensitive, because you have to know that isn't my intent in the least, but I would be remiss if I did not take this opportunity to tell you how you've touched my life. The love and friendship we shared is unmatched by anything I've ever shared with another human being. I loved Derek. I still love Derek with all I have left, he was indeed my brother, but the connection I shared with you is unexplainable.

      A, for what it's worth, I truly am sorry and I'll live with this regret for the rest of my life, eating away at me. If I could take your pain away I'd do it in the blink of an eye. I know too much has happened for us to attempt to salvage anything and unfortunately for us clocks don't operate in reverse, but I do still care about your well-being. I pray that your peace and joy is restored. I will love you forever and am eternally grateful for the time God allowed us to cross paths.

Forever in my heart

A

Alicia

And just like that, I'm made aware that the connection I share with Amir is still as strong as ever. The day after I dropped a letter in the mailbox for him I received a letter of my own. As if he just knew I was reaching out to him, on cue, he reached out to me. Being able to release what I'd been walking around with resting heavy on my spirit and hearing from him has given me a bit of much needed closure.

Today I decided to try to regain some sense of normalcy. One way I know to do that is to do something that once felt normal to me. Something that use to be second nature to me. My solace. My time for meditation. My time to escape the chaos, quiet the noise and gain clarity. I chose to run today. It was a little difficult to pull myself out of bed this morning, but I realized if I'm ever going to move forward I'll have to start putting one foot in front of the other. So I get up and walk slowly, almost stumbling, to the bathroom. I walk over to the sink to brush my teeth when I catch a glimpse of myself in the mirror. I twist the knob for the hot water. "Alicia, you've got to pull yourself together." I splash the warm water on the face. "Today is going to be a good day."

****

Dressed in a pair of black jogging pants and a bright yellow tank top, with my multicolored Adidas Flux. I climb out of my car to begin my run in the park. I questioned whether I should return here. The park being the inception of the end of my world as I once knew it. My accident happened just on the other side of this very park. The accident that took place while I was on the phone with my h... With Amir. The accident that prompted the men I love to both end up at the hospital by my side at the same time. This is the place that use to be my sanctuary. I could come here and center my chi and in the blink of an eye, with a single flap of a butterfly's wing, this place gave birth to a horrific domino effect that sent my life spinning into turmoil. Turmoil I've walked around with for five months. Allowing it to stagger me; to keep me shackled to my grief and guilt. Not moving forward. Not allowing myself to be forgiven. Not believing I deserve forgiveness.

The truth is, I sent those dominoes crashing down the moment I allowed Amir to kiss me. The moment I kissed Amir back. That butterfly flapped it's wings the moment I decided I kissed a boy and I liked it. I chose the park today because I'm taking back my power. Yes, something horrible happened here, but I've had enough great times here to cancel out that tragedy. Yes, a series of tragic events followed that accident in the park that day, but I've been blessed many times over since then. I still have so much to be thankful for.

With my iPod and wireless earbuds set to play India, I am ready. At first I felt a little out of practice; which, if I'm being honest, I was. After a few minutes, my legs felt a little wobbly. My chest and throat began to burn. I was tired. I don't even recognize the girl in the park today. What is happening right now? I came to a bench along the trail. I sat and rested for a couple minutes. Then I decided I should walk for a bit. No need in rushing to run. I'll just walk a bit and when I'm ready, I'll run again. So as India sang, I walked.

Life is a journey, not a destination. There are no mistakes, just chances we've taken. Lay down your regrets cause all we have is now.

Something about those words being spoken in my ear, at this exact moment, made a connection with my spirit.

Wake up in the morning and get out of bed. Start making a mental list in my head of all of the things that I am grateful for.

Confirmation. That's what I'm feeling at this moment. The connection the words of this song has made with my spirit feels like confirmation. Confirmation that I will smile again, and mean it. Confirmation that I will know what it feels like to be happy again. Confirmation that God still loves me and I do deserve forgiveness. I feel in this moment that I can forgive myself. I can grant myself permission to move forward. I find security in knowing that I will enjoy life again. One day. I don't know when that day will find me, but I'm starting today. I forgive myself today. Yes, I've lost so much, but I still have so much to be grateful for. I'm creating new life to bring into the world. I'm healthy. I am loved. Like so many people, I've lost my way. I'm drowning in sorrow and can't tell which way is up. I can't find my way to the surface, but this conflagrative anguish I've been lugging around is temporary. This too shall pass.

Acknowledgements

I came into this only with my love of words and storytelling. There's no way I could have finished this story without the support of my village. I know I spent a lot of time procrastinating and blew through all of the deadlines JB set for me, but I believe I finished exactly when I was supposed to. So to everyone who lent a hand during this process, I genuinely appreciate you. My AMAZING sister Toni, who is constantly reminding me how dope I am and consistently believes in everything I do, without fail, I love you unconditionally. My best friend (the left side of the brain) Deshay, who pushed me relentlessly to get this done all the way until it was time to hit the button, I love you forever. My cousin KeShondra Lyn, who I call on for EVERYTHING, read through my rough draft and gave me her sincerest feedback. Even though you hate the ending (sorry for your loss Krack) thank you for not throwing the whole story away, as we both know is your intuitive reaction when we don't get that ending right. I love and appreciate you INFINITELY!!!

To everyone else who believed in this book, sight unseen, since day one, everyone who helped to push me along when I was stagnant and everyone who selflessly allowed me to bounce ideas off of them, whether it was parts of the book to read, the cover art, whatever, THANK YOU!! THANK YOU!! THANK YOU!!

Made in the USA
Columbia, SC
11 October 2020